I0710537

DIY EXORCISM

BY DAVID WASHBURN

DIY EXORCISM

DAVID WASHBURN

www.washburnwrites.com

DIY Exorcism

© 2024 by David Washburn

All Rights Reserved

No part of this publication may be reproduced, distributed, or transmitted in any form or by any means, including photocopying, recording, or other electronic or mechanical methods, without the prior written permission of the publisher, except as permitted by U.S. copyright law.

This story is a work of fiction.

Any names are a coincidence and locations are fictional aside from the mention of real locations.

Okay ... *maybe* one character is based on an actual person, but that's it!

Cover Design by Grim Poppy Design

Interior Design by Joey Powell/Mad Axe Media

Edited by Kaylynn Wurzelbacher

Published by Burn Ward Publishing

www.WASHBURNWRITES.com

Instagram & Threads: @WashburnWrites

Email: DavidWritesStories@gmail.com

Published in the United States of America.

1 2 3 4 5 6 7 8 9

Dedicated to the strong ones.

Part I

A Performance of Being Human

CHAPTER ONE

Nine o'clock on a Monday evening is not usually *this* tense in the Mitchell household. Dante and Grace have just sent their nine-year-old son, Mason, off to bed not too long ago. They have been bickering and prodding one another all evening, even through dinner, and as they're cleaning up and getting situated for bedtime, they are not ready to wind down just yet.

"Would you just calm down for a second, please?" Dante begs, as he is drying dishes with a hand towel and putting them away. The plates and bowls clank against one another with each aggressive placement.

Grace stands at the kitchen table, folding laundry and placing clothes into a basket. "No, Dante! I am sick and tired of being calm all the time. I'm always the calm one!" She works quickly and seems especially focused despite her tone.

Dante looks over his shoulder. "What is that supposed to mean?"

Grace pulls a few loose strands of her box-blonde hair back and tucks them behind her ears as she closes her eyes with a heavy-winded breath. "I'm always the one here at home with Mason," her voice shakes on the verge of tears, "running him to and from school, church, baseball games, soccer practice, I do it all! I don't have–"

"Now you know I do those same things too. That is not fair!" Dante interrupts, shouting over her.

"Yes, but you are always stressed out about work. The church. The things I'm doing always come after, and I … I just need a break from it sometimes."

"You know what I'm dealing with there trying to keep that place above water! Ever since my dad passed I have been *drowning*!"

Grace's words begin running over Dante's, but he does not waver as they both try talking over one another. "You know if you just could carve out time to spend with us, and maybe not be so … conditional."

"I've got the bills, the special events, I've got a hundred plus people looking at me, not just on Sundays, but *every* single day, and don't get me started on holidays–"

"It's like you only make time out of obligation."

"Obligation!? You think I don't *want* to spend time with you two more!?" Dante whips the towel against the countertop, so hard that it rattles the plates and glasses.

Silence.

Grace stares at Dante with her hands pressed against the rim of the laundry basket on the table. The silence hangs in the air. "I just wish that I felt like you were putting us first sometimes," she says, breaking the silence.

Dante leans against the counter, seething. His head hangs. "What am I supposed to do Grace? Let the church suffer?"

Mason steps into the hallway, their son stands there quietly in his t-shirt and gym shorts. Grace notices and her face softens as she crouches down and opens her arms wide. "Come here, sweetie." He goes to her with his head down and hugs her, laying his head on her shoulder as he looks at his father. "Is everything alright?" she asks.

Dante puts on a happy face, allowing a grin to pull at his cheeks for the sake of Mason, hoping that he didn't understand most of that. "Why do you guys yell at each other?" Mason asks through a soft, yet brave voice.

Dante steps toward the table. "I'm sorry buddy, sometimes grown ups don't always–" Grace sits there on one knee with Mason hanging off of her neck as she motions a finger at Dante to just stop. He stops talking as his eyes dart between his wife and his son.

Grace rubs Mason's back tenderly as she sways back and forth. Her cold gaze pierces through Dante. "I'm only asking for *sometimes*, Dante." She stands up and disappears into the stairwell as she comforts Mason, ushering him to his room.

Dante finishes cleaning up around the kitchen, slamming cabinet doors, and stomping around the house. He decides to step outside to get some fresh air. Stepping outside to breathe has to be better than the thick and uncomfortable air in the house. He grabs a clean, folded hoodie off of the kitchen table and pulls it over his head before stepping outside. As he stands at his back door for a moment, hands in the front pocket of the hoodie, he looks up at the stars and sighs.

"You and the ole lady are really goin' at it in there, huh?" a voice says from the other side of the fence. There sits Barry Hale, in a patio chair in the dark with his feet kicked up on a small table.

Dante is surprised, but glad to see his neighbor outside. "Yeah. Things are a bit ... tense with us right now," he offers.

Barry pulls his feet down and stands up, walking over to the chain-link fence that separates the two men. Barry has become Dante's unofficial confidant over the years. They share views on life in addition to a fence.

Barry takes a drink from his beer can. "I hear ya, I hear ya," he responds. "I don't mean to come off as ... rude, but I got to say, son, I'm a little amused by the irony."

Dante looks at him with an eyebrow raised. "Irony in what?"

Barry leans on the fence and smirks. "The irony ... what could Pastor Mitchell and his gorgeous wife be so at-each-other's throats about?" He takes another sip from the can.

Dante leans against the fence, staring down at his feet, listening to the crickets sing their song while he finds the words. "She tells me that I'm too focused on the church."

"Well ... you're a working man, and the people in this town depend on you."

"She told me tonight that she never feels like I put her first."

"Do you feel like you do?"

"You see, that's the thing. I got so worked up when she said that and in my heart I know that I put her and Mason first ... but when I tried to reason with her ... I don't know, I guess I couldn't really argue."

Barry props himself upright and groans in that way that older men tend to do. "You just need to take the time to remind her that you love her, listen to her, and I mean *really* listen to her."

Dante nods in agreement. "Mason asked her tonight why we fight so much. I didn't know what to say. Grace stopped me. She's had enough. I feel like I'm screwing this up."

"Kind of funny." Barry takes another drink and tosses the empty can over his shoulder and it lands near the trash can on the sidewalk. "The bright light that everyone comes to for their own issues, the pastor," he gestures to the sky with both hands spanning wide, "voice of God, whatever ... you have problems just like everyone else."

Dante raises his eyebrows and sighs. "Well, I'm still human."

"Amen," he says with a chuckle. "Amen."

Dante looks at the stars. "I should probably head back inside, I'll talk to you later."

"Just remember to breathe, everything'll be alright."

"Goodnight, Barry."

"Goodnight, Pastor."

Dante strolls back into the house with a clearer head. He sees Grace sitting in a dark living room and sits beside her. She hides a face made of stone so Dante doesn't see the tear streaks. Years of enduring stress and pent up feelings hide in those roads paved by tears on her face.

"What's the matter?" Dante asks.

She does not answer him.

Grace sniffles, fighting back tears as she leans into him. They sit on the couch as the silence clings to the air. She lies her head on his shoulder as he embraces her with his arm. "I think we should take some time."

Dante's arm pulls away and he scoots back, only to get a good, full look at her. Stunned, he struggles to match his thoughts to his words. "I ... I think we should at least try to fix–"

"There is nothing to try now, Dante," Grace interrupts, with confidence, and finality. "I've tried talking. I've tried being patient. I've been thinking about this for a few months now."

"A few months!?" Dante says, trying to keep his voice down so as not to wake their son. He stands, beginning to pace the living room floor. "Why didn't you bring this up sooner?"

Grace's jaw hangs. "Sooner? All I've been doing is reaching for you and trying to get you to just be more present with us–"

"You don't think maybe we should see a counselor or something, maybe we can–"

"It's over Dante. I'm just ... done."

Dante plops down onto the couch and cradles his face into his hands. He looks up, feeling as if the walls were suddenly closing in. His heart flutters as the heat rushes through his face. "What am I supposed to tell people?"

Grace hesitates, letting her words come together thoughtfully. "Tell them whatever you need to, Dante."

"We're supposed to be a symbol. I'm the pastor. Do you have any idea how this looks if our marriage fails?"

Grace stares back at Dante, stunned and wearing a smirk. "This is exactly the problem."

"What?"

"What you just said. You're worried about what the people around town see and think. I need my husband to be worried about what *I* see and think." She catches herself nearly yelling and lowers her volume. "I need my husband to be worried about what his *son* sees and thinks. What kind of man are you?"

Dante's looks at her, fighting back tears. "I'm trying to be a man of God. Let me fix this."

"There's nothing to fix!"

"How can you not be willing to at least try?"

"I'm done trying."

"Well I'm not!" His head is spinning and he doesn't know what else he can say. *She is right about everything.* He recognizes the time he should have been focusing on his home and not everybody else's. Her words sink into his mind with his world beginning to crack beneath him. All of the times she was reaching for him, he only wishes he would've been reaching back.

"We can still make this work and it doesn't have to be a bad thing," Grace stammers through a weak voice. "Sometimes two people just grow apart and need to know when to call it ... I'm sorry, Dante."

CHAPTER TWO

SUNDAY

Fifteen months later.

Dante stands at a small podium from a modest stage that is a couple steps up, in the front of the church. Dante Mitchell, pastor of the Heart of Our Savior church, is warming up, ready to provide his Sunday sermon to the members of the New Richmond community that loyally attend every week to listen to his words. His eyes scan the pews that go all the way back to the main entrance, ten rows of them with a walkway down the middle, and about half of the seating is occupied this morning. Families from nearby flock to the gospel and others, simply for the community that comes with it.

"Today, I want you to open your Bibles to 1 Peter 5:7, which says this: Casting all of your care upon Him, for He careth for you." Dante paces the stage slowly as he speaks. "Now ... what does this mean? *How does this make me feel? How does this speak to my soul?* You might be asking yourself."

Dante stops and stares into the pews for a moment. Many faces he recognizes. Many friends and folks who he has known for a long time. "I want to tell you what this passage says to me today. A couple days ago, I was at the grocery store, picking up some things, small trip, nothing extravagant on my end. I go to the checkout and I am standing there in line, captive to my surroundings while I wait. I'm standing there and there is this woman in front of me. Younger than me probably, she has a cart full of things and she is trying to move her stuff from the cart to the belt while trying to engage in polite banter with the cashier."

Dante paces to the other side of the stage, well dressed as he commands the room with his influence and respected voice. "I also happened to notice her baby that was feet-a-swingin' in the shopping cart. The child was being fussy and this woman is trying to be attentive to her baby while doing all of this. On top of that, she also has two older boys. Maybe five, six, maybe seven years old. One boy is standing on the side of the cart while she asks him to stop climbing. The other boy is standing there, begging for candy bars. All while the cashier is asking if she has a reward card, and a myriad of other questions.

"Now, this woman was obviously dealing with a lot there. I am sure many of you can relate, being a parent can sometimes feel like a circus performance. Juggling from one thing to the next and nothing being perfect. In this moment, I saw her for what she was. A person who was trying. Someone who needed a break. A win!" Dante's voice becomes boisterous with his passionate speech. "This lady, I could tell, hadn't taken the time to fix herself up. She wasn't going out for a hot date on a Tuesday afternoon but she was still beautiful. The cashier rings her up, gives her her total and in a moment of me trying to be my best self, I stepped up and offered to pay for her groceries. I didn't mind. I could see that she was dealing with a lot. Still though, she smiled politely," his voice lowers and becomes playful, "maybe a little uncomfortably if I'm being honest." The attendees laugh. "She tells me *that is very kind, but no, I've got it.*"

Dante raises his hands and smirks with stretched lips. "I don't press the issue, I ask if she is sure and she proceeds to thank me for the gesture as she unfurls cash and uncrumpled balls of money from her clutch. As the cashier tells her to have a nice day, I step up and I tell her God bless and she goes on with her day. I go on with mine."

Dante steps back to the podium, "Now the Bible says we can cast our cares on Him, but sometimes, much like the woman in the grocery store, we think we can do it all. What 1 Peter 5:7 is telling us is that, if you need help, let Jesus know. The Lord will take on your burdens. Your stress. He will lighten your load and make sure to put you where you need to be."

He focuses on the many faces, seeing the message sitting with them. He sees his son, Mason, swinging his feet and picking at the splinters on the lip of the seating as he slouches into the wooden pews looking as uncomfortable as a person can look. His mother, Grace, is to his right, looking ahead, attentive to the message. Dante locks eyes with her for only a moment. Dante stands there, sinking in the sea of dark water that are his thoughts while remembering her soft features and warm smile. After all this time, since the split he still grieves the failure of their union under God, similar to how you might grieve someone who has died. In some ways, he believes a part of him did die that night when she said it was over. Living with her for so long after that was an exercise in inner strength for him as he felt like some days were closer to healing while other days were like living with the corpse of his past self.

Beside Grace sits Karl, her new boyfriend, who only recently began attending the church with her.

Because of her.

With the dissolution being finalized recently and still fresh, it offers a newfound freedom for the two to go on with their lives. Still being tied to one another through a child, and the church that Grace is still a very active member of. Dante has held it together to be civil and pretend he isn't hurt.

Grace grabs Karl's hand and they both sit closely. Karl appears to be active, he's good-looking, tall, and maybe a little younger than Grace. Dante has met him already and spoken with him a few times and he is a respectful and genuinely nice guy. Dante isn't worried about her dating, so long as Mason is happy and well taken care of by all of the adults in his life.

He realizes as he watches their hand-holding that he has stopped talking and he has to talk himself out of this trance, in front of an audience.

"Sorry, where was I?" Dante laughs at himself. "I swear, I'd lose my head if it wasn't attached." Most of the people in attendance find it amusing as well, with a few hearty laughs. "Well," he says, stretching the word as he thinks of what to say next. "All you have to do is pray, talk to Jesus, acknowledge you can't do it all yourself. He loves you and us mortals weren't meant to carry the weight alone."

Dante's eyes fall back on Grace and Karl's hands clasped together. Fingers interlocking in a way that he misses. "Let us pray."

After the prayer, much of the crowd makes their exit. Dante steps off of the stage and shares words with members of the church for about twenty minutes before catching up with Grace. Mason and Karl are off to the side as Mason is showing Karl a complicated looking handshake.

"Good sermon," Grace says, offering a smirk.

He smiles, hanging his head. "Thank you." He looks past Grace and watches Mason laugh at something Karl must have said. "So, you guys heading out?"

"Yeah, are you still okay to take Mason to your place from here?"

"Of course, no problem."

"Great," she says, turning to Mason. "Come over here, say bye, your dad is going to take you home and I'll see you later, okay?"

Mason hustles over to her and gives her a big hug. "Okay Mom," he says, pulling away quickly.

The two parents watch as he runs outside to join some of the other kids playing on the swingset. "I love you!" Grace shouts.

"Love you, too!" he replies back, with a wave of his arm and his back to her.

Grace walks away and joins Karl, looping an arm under his. Dante watches for a brief moment before he realizes he is staring too hard. He heads back inside to wrap some things up while Mason hangs outside.

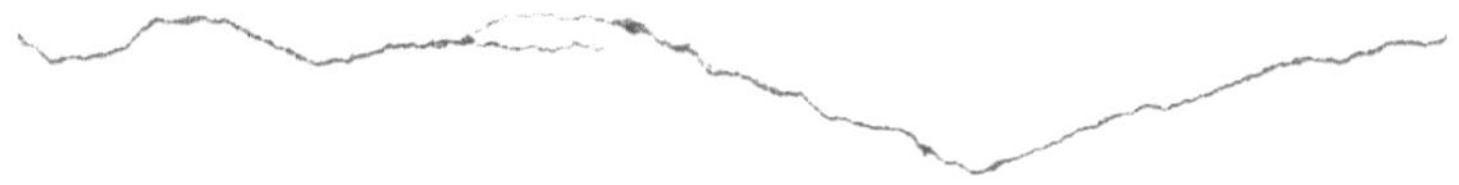

Dante sits at his desk in the back office with the door shut, leaning back in a pleather office chair, spacing out with his eyes on a stack of bills. Tapping an ink pen against his cheek as the chair whines from him rocking, he knows that those bills aren't being paid by the community tithe alone and managing things in the church have been challenging to say the least.

The Police and Fire departments do well to help with events, but in the past year the church has organized less events and it is all due to Dante's inexperience with this aspect of the church. His eyes crawl across the table and land on a small frame with a picture of his father. Since his father passed away, he was the next in line to take care of things. The pen cap finds its way between his teeth as he studies the photo. Giving sermons and being a friend to the people in New Richmond was one thing, but he never expected—or planned—to be *the* head pastor at Heart of Our Savior. Not after his dad was the face for so many years. Even doing it for this short time felt weird. It was like wearing a suit tailored for someone else.

People whisper and Dante sometimes catches bits and pieces of more colorful opinions on how he does things differently than his dad. Some of the folks who still volunteer have accepted Dante, but they make sure to find little indirect ways to remind him that he isn't his father.

"Pastor Dante," a voice beckons outside the door, followed by knocking. The door opens and Susan comes in before he can even answer. "Pastor Dante, Mister Patrick and Miss Brenda are asking about the luncheon next Sunday and if it is still happening."

She stares at him, eager for a response. Dante stops rocking and puts the pen on the desk as he leans forward. His nose and forehead scrunch up. "Is there a reason why it wouldn't be happening still?"

"Well I don't know, sometimes plans fall apart."

"Yes Susan, the luncheon is still happening next Sunday."

Susan's eyes open wide to this revelation with a single hand surrendering as she eases backwards out the door. "Okay, that's what I thought, I was just checkin'."

The door pulls shut and he sits there letting out an airy chuckle. He straightens up the desk and gets up, but as he is going to the door, he stops. Susan is nearby talking to someone. He hears his name and her familiar annoyed tone and can't help but to wait, curious of what she has to say. He leans his ear closer to the door.

"I'm not saying he is bad, but his father ran things so much smoother," Susan says.

An unknown voice offers minimal to the conversation from what Dante can hear.

"Pastor Dante is a sweetheart and he can talk a good game, but this place really needs someone more like his dad," she says, with a little attitude in her voice.

Dante pulls away from the door like hot steel kissing his ear at the mention of his father. Frustration mounts as he waits for them to clear the hallway so he can leave without feeling awkward.

Chapter Three

The summer afternoon sun blankets Dante and Mason's faces in the front seat of the car. With one hand on the wheel, Dante leads them home.

"So, are you playing any games lately, buddy?" Dante asks.

Mason fiddles with his tablet, mindlessly entranced, as he ignores father.

Dante's eyes shift from the road to study his son. "Whatcha watchin' there?" he asks, cutting through the silence.

"Mr. Beast," the boy replies, with his eyes glued to the small screen.

"Who is that?"

"He streams Minecraft," Mason answers.

"Like, he just plays the game?" Dante questions.

"Yeah. He's funny."

"You have this game, right?" Dante asks, perplexed.

"Mhm."

Dante's eyebrow pulls up his face, "So why don't you just play it?"

Mason shrugs with his bottom lip puckered out. "I don't know. I like to watch and see what kind of stuff he does. He's funny."

A soft cackle breaks through Dante's mouth with a smile and a head shake. "Ain't that something. When I was a boy, playing the game was plenty of fun. Now kids are watching other people play the game when they could be playing it. What a time to be alive."

"What kinda games did you play?" Mason asks, breaking his attention from the tablet, but only because of an advertisement that can't be skipped.

"Well," Dante begins. "Street Fighter, Mario, games like that."

"Were they fun?"

"They were until they weren't. It was nice having a buddy to play with, but I mostly liked going outside and playing ball or exploring ... Do you ever go outside?"

Mason sits silently, like he knows the truth to that question won't be the right answer.

"You should put the game down, get outside once in a while, buddy," Dante suggests.

"I do! When we go swimming," Mason retorts.

With a head nod of approval from Dante, "Okay, well I guess that is better than no sunshine." Extended silence joins the conversation. Dante reaches for anything to keep talking with his son, "So ... are you excited for the luncheon next Sunday? After church."

"Yes!" Mason perks up. "Karl is going to bring his Batman figures to show me."

A deep breath suppresses an unkind reaction to the mention of Karl. "Batman, huh? You like superheroes?"

Mason's face lights up. "Yeah. Batman is my favorite now."

"Tell you what, why don't next weekend I take you to go see the new Justice League movie?"

"I already saw it," Mason says.

"You did?" Dante asks, with a layer of surprise in his voice.

"Mhm, Mom and Karl took me."

"Oh," Dante says, as his face loses expression and a new layer of betrayal taints his voice. "I see."

The hurt, the jealousy, the pain inside his heart, the stress that's on his mind every waking moment of each day can sometimes feel like a juggling act. Which ball will he drop first? Dealing with the shared parenting since Grace and him had split has been an emotional hardship, to put it lightly. Despite still being present and active in Mason's life and seeing him regularly, he still clings onto opportunities to feel close to his son.

"Can we get McDonald's?" a very spirited Mason asks.

The excitement and pure goodness of his boy was enough to dissipate those feelings, if only for a moment. Dante grins as he glances over at Mason who awaits the answer. "Sure, kiddo. Let's eat," he replies as he tousles Mason's hair.

"Can I get a Happy Meal?" he asks, even more excited.

"Of course," Dante says. "Maybe we can grab some fudge sundaes too, how 'bout it?"

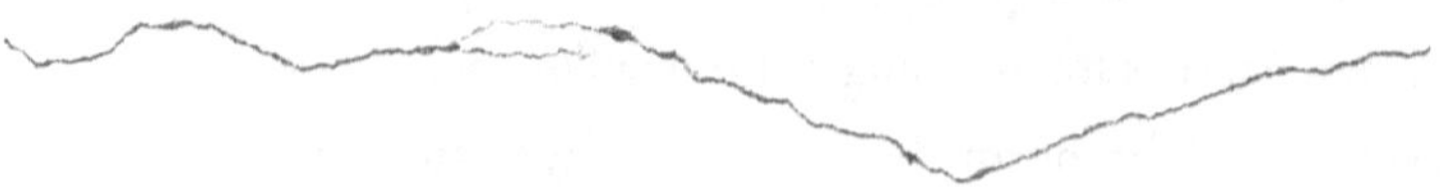

Dante and Mason pull into the driveway with fast food for lunch and the rest of the day to themselves. The house is a modest, single-family, two-story dwelling with a sizable covered porch, respectable landscaping, and a large front-facing window that overlooks the sidewalk between the driveway and front porch.

Mason runs to the front door and waits for his dad to catch up and unlock it. Dante comes up the stairs with the key ready, a McDonald's bag and a Happy Meal box in his hands, with a messenger bag pulling at his shoulder.

"Here you go, buddy," he says, handing Mason his food.

"Thank you!" he says, eager to get inside and open it to see what kind of toy is waiting between his fries and nuggets.

The front door opens, Mason runs inside, through the living room, to the dining room table. Dante follows, stopping in the foyer next to the stairs. There are three bedrooms even though there's just the two of them and the extra room full of things from a previous chapter in their life. The main floor and kitchen are shared with the open dining room and living space, but plenty of room.

"Make sure you wash your hands first," Dante says as he tosses his keys into a dish on the kitchen counter.

He sets his bag on his computer desk that is in the dining room. A small desk with a small work space, big enough for just himself. He wastes no time to open the laptop and logs onto the church's Facebook account. Every day Dante has been reliable for sharing a motivational video with the friends and followers of the church in this space. Typically he will post this onto Instagram as well afterward.

Dante's face pops up on the screen, a clean white dress shirt with his sleeves rolled up as he prepares to record. Behind him you can see the kitchen cabinets and part of the refrigerator.

He presses the *record* icon.

"Hey there everybody," he starts, waving with a gleaming smile. "So, I am just getting home today, I've got Mason here with me and we are about to eat some ... fast food," he chuckles to himself as he crosses his arms and leans forward onto the desk. "The Lord blesses us with nourishment and today it happens to be cheeseburgers and fries."

"And ice cream!" Mason shouts from the table just out of frame.

Dante laughs, turning to Mason with a wink and back to the camera with bright blue eyes that steal the show. "And ice cream, that's right, buddy."

Dante takes a moment to let the laughter fade.

"I just want to thank those of you who attended today to hear the message. It is appreciated and as always, I am so happy and proud to be a part of this community and fortunate enough to be someone you all trust. I am grateful that I can be counsel when you need it and every day I thank God that this town can come together and support one another in times of need. It is truly something special. When I tell you that the members of this church are like one big family, it isn't an exaggeration. I will keep it short and sweet today."

He looks away from the camera for a moment.

"How's the food?" he asks Mason.

"My fries are cold," he says.

Dante smirks. "Yeah, that happens sometimes."

He looks back into the camera. "So if you happen to have missed this morning's message, I thought it was a good one to mention here because I think it is important for everyone to hear. If you open your Bible and reference 1 Peter 5:7, it says: *Casting all of your care upon Him; For He careth for you.* I won't get all into the story I shared this morning, but basically this means that if you talk to God, harness a relationship with Jesus, that no matter what problems you're facing, no matter what burdens or stressors you have, you can always ask God for help. He loves you and does not want you to suffer. Remember, next Sunday we're having the luncheon after the morning service. I would love to see everybody there. I'll be back tomorrow with more positivity. Goodbye for now and God bless."

Dante signs off and posts the video. He has done this routinely for a few years, even when his dad was still around and handling more of the church's upkeep. Dante used to just deliver a short sermon and help out. These motivational videos he does daily were sort of a fun thing he enjoyed when he didn't feel like he was being pulled in six directions at once. The followers have come to expect these little videos and seem to be really engaged in them, which was one of the things his father always spoke highly of when it came to his contributions to the church.

His father's absence has put his shortcomings and strengths in perspective. Just one more ball in the juggler's act.

CHAPTER FOUR

D ante wolfs down his burger and cold fries before he stands at the sink, washing the few dishes there are. He notices through the window, his neighbor Barry is grilling. The smell of overcooked beef wafts just past the window, managing to seep through somewhere despite the windows being closed. The aroma is enough to lure Dante out as he cleans up and takes the kitchen trash out through the back door.

"Howdy neighbor!" Barry shouts, as Dante hauls the bag to the can.

"Hey!" Dante replies. "Good afternoon."

"I was just about to throw some dogs on, ya hungry?"

"I just ate," Dante replies, in an effort to resist, "but thank you."

"You sure? I got burgers too."

"Yeah, I thought that's what I smelled burning," Dante jabs.

Barry shakes his head with a mischievous smile as he holds the cover open to the grill and rotates hot dogs over the fire. "Funny guy. Who told you that one? Jesus?"

Dante leans on the fence, his face lit up after Barry's quip. "He did, actually. He asked me to make sure that it isn't anyone's last supper."

Barry closes the grill and smoke billows thick around it. His cheeks glow red and raise as his smile stretches across his face. "You are somethin' else, neighbor, you know that?"

"So you tell me."

Barry leans on the fence between the two men. He lets out a hearty grunt, "So how are things going with Grace?"

Dante's lip pulls to one side with a squint. "As fine as they can be, I guess."

"You guess?"

Dante exhales. "She's been bringing her new boyfriend around lately."

Barry marinates in the silence while he reaches for meaningful words. "It's been a year, right?" Barry asks. "Maybe more?"

"Yeah," Dante says, elongating the response. "I guess I just didn't anticipate us moving on for good."

"You expected her to wait around forever?"

"No," Dante says. "I just– I ... I don't know."

"Well, did you ask God?" Barry asks through a playful grin. "Maybe Jesus can hook you up with one of them seventy-two virgins or somethin'."

Dante lets out a snicker. "I think you're getting your religions a bit twisted, my friend."

"Agggh," Barry groans. "Well, talk to me, neighbor, things with Mason seem to be going okay. He looks like he is happy as a clam. What's *really* troubling you?"

Dante looks at Barry, as he stands on the other side of the fence. Barry spins a can of beer in his hands as they talk. Dante is reluctant to open up, although it hasn't stopped him before. Barry is a slick-talking police officer who is trustworthy and has become a close friend and sounding board to Dante.

"I guess I just feel a little lost, if I'm being honest."

Barry steps back with a shocked grin. "Lost? Aren't you supposed to be the holy man?"

Dante fixes his sight on the smoke that seeps from the grill. "Yeah, yeah, I know … this split between Grace and I, having all of the church operations fall in my lap, having all of these people depending on me … it's just a lot sometimes."

"Don't you have people there you can delegate things to?"

"I do, but some things I need to do myself."

"You don't trust your people?"

"It's not that … I guess what I am hemmin' and hawin' about is that, if I am being honest with myself, I don't know that I seen myself being a head pastor."

"You know, the good thing is that you can quit and go be something else if you want to."

"Yeah, but I guess I'm ashamed … like I'm letting the people down."

"I get it, neighbor … let me ask you this," Barry says, opening the can of beer and taking a sip. He pulls it away and wipes the foam from his goatee using his forearm. "What would you do if you didn't have all that shame?"

"I think I would still want to help people in some way. Maybe just not be the main person all the time that everyone is running to for a prayer."

Barry's face lights up. "Ever consider being a fireman or police officer?"

Dante only offers a laugh.

"I'm serious, neighbor. You're still young enough to apply. It's of service to the community. I see how you have such a hard-on for that sorta thing, and it puts you on a team of other like-minded people."

"Hmm," Dante ponders. He had never thought very seriously of being anything other than in his father's shadow, but Barry is dishing out the hard truths that Dante has come to admire in his neighbor.

"Listen, I know I give you a lot of shit, pardon my French, but you're a good person, obviously ... you already have the respect of the community and this is a noble and selfless job too. All you're doing is switching lanes."

"You make it hard to argue."

"Look, if you're serious about this, I can get some information together for you during the week and maybe put a bug in the right ears." Barry takes another sip.

Dante lets the thought sit with him for a moment. Leaving the church has never been something he has ever actively tried to do, but all of a sudden the burdens, weights, and ideas of doing something for himself feel a whole world lighter. While he loves what he does, he has always struggled to shake the feeling that he is just following a path his father made. The possibility of Dante making his own way is more real than it has ever seemed. Stepping out of the old man's shadow is as appealing as it is exciting, but just as overwhelming. Letting his father down was never the goal, and feeling like his father is looking down on him and disappointed is an added weight. Leaving the church to someone else is a tall task of its own.

"You think I'm cut out for police work? Seriously?" Dante asks.

Barry goes over to the grill and opens the lid and begins to rotate some hot dogs. "I wouldn't offer to co-sign for you if I didn't." He begins to take the meat off the grill and puts them onto a plate. "Besides, somethin' about a pastor with a police-issued firearm is hilarious to me."

"Well ... I think I might just want to do this." Dante grins with a nod. "It's time that I ... shoot my shot."

Barry laughs. "Gun pun?"

Dante smiles. "Gun pun."

Chapter Five

Dante comes back into the house and is met with Mason standing in the kitchen with an oversized cowboy hat on, leering. A plastic gold sheriff's badge speaks to the authority from the pin in his shirt that Barry gave him some time recently. He postures in his socks with the brim of the hat between his finger and thumb and the other hand hovering over the toy pistol with the orange-tipped barrel that is tucked into his waistband.

"I thought I told you not to come into my town again," Mason says through a gravelly and forced voice that barely hides a smile that wants to break free.

Dante stops in motion and raises his hands. "Howdy, Sheriff, funny I should be seeing you here."

Mason takes a couple steps toward his father and draws the gun quickly and points, "Where's the money!? I know you and your bandits hi-jacked that train."

"I'll never tell!" Dante bursts off running around the dining room table. With the fresh ideas of a career change in mind, this game that they're played for years suddenly has a new context. Mason wears the badge, but maybe Dante can too.

Mason gives chase, round and round as he pulls the trigger, the hammer snaps loud in unison with the gun sounds he makes with his mouth. "Get back here, you have to go to jail!"

"You'll never take me alive!" Dante grabs an apple from the bowl in the center of the table and rolls it across the table at Mason. It hits his shoulder and Mason laughs hysterically for just a moment, stopping briefly before going back into super-serious-sheriff-mode.

The chase continues and the plastic cowboy revolver has clicked at least a dozen times now. Dante doesn't mind letting Mason fire more shots than the gun can actually fire. As long as Mason is smiling and having fun, Dante would let him fire a million fake shots.

Dante slows down and sits for just a moment, long enough to allow the sheriff of Mason's imaginary dining room town to catch up to him and press the end of the gun into his lower back. "I got you!" Mason squeals, firing the gun three more times. "You're going to jail now!"

Dante can't help but to laugh. "How am I going to go to jail if you shoot me to death?"

Mason only laughs, grabbing Dante's wrist and pulling his arm down, "Doesn't matter. Let's go, robber!"

Mason leads Dante through the door that goes from the dining room, down the steps to the laundry room in the basement. A dungeon of slate gray pairs well with the faint damp smell that hits his nose as he touches the top step. Dante is careful with his foot falls on each step, as the lighting isn't the greatest in the hallway. The basement is not finished and primarily used for laundry, the HVAC system, and additional storage.

"Not much of a jail. Is this where you keep all of the baddies?" Dante asks. Warm light glows softly from exposed light sockets that hang on opposite ends.

"That's enough out of you!" Mason demands, pulling a little harder on Dante down the stairs. The HVAC system is large and sits along the adjoining wall with pipes coming from all sides of it, and a cast-iron drain pipe that feeds into the floor.

On the pipe, a glimmering pair of carbon steel long handcuffs hang open, waiting for their next criminal. Officer Barry has always been such a nice guy and even better neighbor. He has taken a liking to Mason and known him since he was in diapers. Over the years he has made a habit out of giving Mason cool stuff that most kids may not get exposed to. Toy guns, police badges, smoke bombs, and most recently, police grade ankle cuffs that he showed Mason how to use. Of course, Dante has one of the extra keys.

Every weekend since they got them, Mason has sparked up these games of good guy versus bad guy in the house and ultimately, Dante is led into the *jail cell*, and arrested. Left to sit in the poor lighting, on cold concrete, with limited movement. Mason is growing up and Dante finds it a bit odd that Mason still plays these kinds of games around the house with his pops. With Mason being the only child, Dante finds himself trying to hang onto these moments as long as he can, so he is happy to be the criminal in any game his little boy wants to play with him.

Mason grabs his dad's arm and the open cuff and tries to wriggle them on. "Okay, now you're gonna sit there until you tell me where the money is."

The steel bangs and scrapes against the pipe with each little movement. "I'll never tell, and soon my crew will come and bust me out of here."

Mason secures Dante to the pipe and walks to the bottom of the stairs and turns back, dramatically. "Tell it to the hangman!"

He runs up the steps, the thuds echoing before the door is shut to the basement and the silence is only met with Dante's own breathing. Dante reaches into his pocket and pulls out a set of keys. The jangling of the keys and the rattling of the cuffs dancing along the pipe. He maneuvers creating a symphony performed by awful musicians with the worst instruments as he cringes with every searing scraping of metal on metal. Dante is able to release himself in a short time and the criminal has escaped his cell.

CHAPTER SIX

Later in the evening Dante is dishing up a serving of Cincinnati-style chili spaghetti for Mason. He likes it with just cheese, while Dante serves himself up a larger plate, fully loaded with cheese, onions, hot sauce, and a fistful of oyster crackers.

He sets the food on the dining table. "Mason!" he hollers. "Dinner's ready!"

"Okay!" he replies, his voice echoing from upstairs. "Be right there! I just need five minutes."

With a sigh, Dante walks over to the bottom of the steps. "Come on, buddy. Come eat with me. You don't want it gettin' cold, do ya?" he shouts into the stairwell.

"Just ten minutes!" Mason responds, with an edge to his voice.

"You just said *five*," Dante says in jest. Lingering near the bottom step, he hears Mason playing a video game. Light atmospheric music rings through the upstairs hallway accompanied by explosion sounds and Mason mashing buttons, audibly frustrated.

Dante walks away shaking his head, allowing Mason more time to come down for dinner. This version of Mason, the growing boy with burgeoning testosterone that threatens to fire him off into puberty any second has Dante a little nervous. It is easy to reflect on his own childhood, but his situation was much different than Mason's. Dante didn't grow up in a broken home.

Before Dante has his seat, he goes to the kitchen sink where he keeps his medication nearby. He grabs a clean pint glass, fills it halfway with water, twists off the lid to the bottle and swallows the pills. *Down the hatch,* he thinks. Afterward he has a seat on a wooden bar stool that sits along the counter. Dante has been practicing different forms of meditation in the past year. Since the break from Grace, he sought out therapy, if only for the private counsel to deal with his most private thoughts. Dr. Bryant has been a huge advocate and support system through what was a turbulent point for the entire family.

With his eyelids relaxed and shut, he loosens his shoulders and sits upright. A big gulping inhale through his nose, and a long deflated exhale through his mouth. Nowadays he is finding this to be helpful throughout the day. Where others have come to Dante for guidance, he has turned to these moments to just breathe and re-center himself. This goes on for five minutes before he goes over again and hollers up the steps. "Mason, come eat!"

Mason grunts, muttering things under his breath. Dante hears the controller slam as Mason stomps out of his room and down the stairs.

Dante stares at him as he storms past him and heads to the table. "What's going on, son?"

Mason pulls the chair out. "I wasn't done playing my game yet."

"Well, I called for you a while ago to come eat," Dante says.

"I'm not hungry," Mason argues.

Dante stares, unsure how to parent this. "Okay ... do you want something else?"

Mason crosses his arms and his expression is seething rage. He shakes his head *no.*

Dante has a seat in front of his (now cold) chili, and leans back in his chair, spinning a fork between his finger and thumb, staring at

Mason while he tugs on his bottom lip with his teeth. "You know what, I think if that game is going to make you this upset, maybe it's time to turn it off."

Mason's jaw drops, along with his arms. "What!?" he shouts, with a whine to his voice. "You can't do that!"

"If it's gonna make you so angry that you won't eat your food and it's got you," Dante leans onto the table, gesturing at Mason with the fork, "like this...then yes, yes I *can* do that."

With an aggressive scoot, Mason pulls his body to the table and picks up his fork, nostrils flaring, failing to mask his agitation. He stares at his dad as he twists the spaghetti onto his fork.

"You got something you wanna say to me, son?"

Mason's eyes tear through Dante. He lets go of the fork and lets it bang against the table. "Mom and Karl let me come to dinner whenever I'm ready."

"Okay," Dante begins, leaning closer. The mention of things being different with his mom makes Dante feel somehow like a bad parent. The mention of Karl's name in the same sentence as 'Mom' coming from Mason's lips makes him feel incredibly inadequate. "In this house though, we eat dinner together, like we always have."

Mason continues his piercing glare, "But if I don't want to eat, then I'm just sitting here," he says, through gritted teeth.

Dante scrunches his nose and shrugs in the universal 'I don't know' position, "I guess then you're just gonna watch me eat while I try to have a conversation with you."

"Karl doesn't make me come to–" Mason's voice raises.

Dante's fist pounds the table. "Karl isn't your father, I am!" Mason flinches and his demeanor morphs into immediate obedience as he tries to hide the look of surprise on his face. "I am your father."

Mason stares at his father, his chest rising and deflating rapidly. He looks away and scoots closer to the table, beginning to eat his dinner. The silence lingers heavy in the air. Forks scraping plates and drinking glasses thudding against the wooden surface after each drink as the two say nothing at all, long enough for it to be plenty uncomfortable.

Dante clears his plate and leans back, staring at his empty glass. The words assemble in his mouth thoughtfully and it shows in his face. "I'm sorry I raised my voice."

Mason sits frozen with unspoken questions in his eyes.

"Why don't you go back upstairs?" Dante suggests rising from the table he reaches for Mason's plate. "I'll get cleaned up, maybe we can watch a movie or you can show me what you've been playing up there."

Mason eases out of his chair, quiet as a mouse as he sneaks away. Dante tends to the dinner clean up. After a few moments he dries his hands off and reaches for his phone.

He composes a new text message, with Grace as the recipient.

19:36

Hey

GRACE
19:37

Hi Dante, what's going on?

19:37

Everything is fine. I just wanted to let you know something happened here a little while ago.

GRACE
19:40

Oh God, is Mason alright? Do you need me to come over?

19:41

No, no, no need to come over. I just raised my voice at him and I think I scared him a little.

GRACE
19:41

What did you yell at him about?

19:42

It's not a big deal. I shouldn't have yelled at him.

19:42

I was telling him dinner was ready and to come down stairs and he kept playing the game.

19:42

Then he started getting upset and stomped downstairs.

19:42

He was back-talking and being very rude and when I told him we eat together he told me you and Karl let him do whatever. [19:43] I slammed my hand on the table and told him we eat dinner together in this house and I just think maybe it has been a long day. I told him I was sorry though but I just wanted to tell you. Just in case it came up.

GRACE
19:45

Wow. Well I'm sure he will be fine. You don't have to be so upset with yourself. It's okay to be mad every so often. Sounds like he was being a brat.

19:47

I still feel bad about it.

GRACE
19:48

I think if you just sleep it off you will be better in the morning. Same for him. Do you want me to come get him?

19:49

No. That's alright. I'm sure you're right. I just feel bad is all. Don't you worry about it. Enjoy your evening. I love you.

GRACE
19:50

Have a good night. Get some rest. Mason will get over it quicker than you know it. Take care of yourself.

The response doesn't sting as much as Grace ignoring him after letting another *I love you* slip. An old habit that still exists. Just as embarrassed as the last time he did it, he puts the phone down on his bedside table and plugs in the charger. He hovers outside of Mason's bedroom and observes uncomfortable air.

It is quiet.

He considers knocking but Grace's wisdom echoes back to him in his mind. *Mason will get over it quicker than you know it.* She is probably right, he knows, but it doesn't do much to alleviate the guilt he feels at the moment. He resists the urge to knock and risk making things worse, deciding to sleep it off and let cooler heads prevail.

CHAPTER SEVEN

THURSDAY

During the week, Mason is primarily with his mother. She takes him to and from school while Dante assists as needed. Usually in the afternoon though, duties with the church can keep him tied up and at times a bit unreliable. Finding time for therapy has been an adjustment in the last year but Dante finds that the option of not having to go into an office is quite convenient.

Every other Thursday, at one o'clock in the afternoon, Dante opens his laptop and clicks on a video link to have a virtual office visit with his therapist, Dr. Bryant. Dante sits in his office at the church with the door shut while he watches the screen. His mirrored-self stares back at him on the screen while he watches the words to the meeting dance along the screen. *This meeting will begin shortly.* In the chat window, off to the side, it shows that little green dot indicating Dr. Bryant is now online. Relief settles over Dante as he waits anxiously for the doctor's digital arrival.

It is not long before the speaker chimes and a familiar face with a bald head and black frame glasses shuffles onto the screen. He is adjusting himself and too close to the computer as he gets situated. "Good afternoon, Dante, sorry I'm late," he says, with a soft-spoken, calming voice that rings evident of education and level-headedness.

"It's no problem at all, actually, I don't think you're technically late. You're right on time," Dante informs.

Dr. Bryant positions the computer on his end, finally framing him decently as he sits back in his office chair. "Well, I always say," he begins, "being on time is late, and being early is on time, so ... boy, it has been a crazy day."

Dante laughs, not because he is amused, but maybe a little bit of him not knowing how to contribute to the small talk. "I hear ya."

The doctor lets out a loud exhale, interlacing his fingers and resting on his desk as he leans forward, "So how's Dante doing this week? Anybody given' ya grief?"

"Well when you put it like that," Dante starts. He leans back in his chair and stares away from the computer. "Where do I start?"

"Well, don't overthink it, just say what's on your mind right now, maybe."

Dante took in a deep breath before he brought Dr. Bryant up to speed on what happened at dinner the other night, from Mason being sassy to how Dante snapped and yelled.

"Well, if he was being sassy, parents sometimes yell, that's not all *that* unusual."

"I like to think I am pretty good about *not* yelling at my son."

"Do you feel guilty?"

"Very."

"Hmmm," the therapist taps his finger on his wedding ring. "What kind of sass was Mason giving you that warranted that reaction?"

"I was asking him to come eat dinner with me. He made a fuss about it because he was playing his game."

"That doesn't sound unlike children his age, if I'm being honest."

"When he eventually came to dinner, he made a stink and mentioned that his mother and her new boyfriend, Karl, don't make him eat with them ... I think hearing him mention Grace's new boyfriend and seeing him at church recently has–"

"Got you on edge?" the doctor interrupts. "Insecure, possibly?"

The space between them hangs calm. Dante connects the dots to these obvious call outs that were a little oblivious to him prior. "I guess it's possible ... I was giving the sermon this past Sunday and he was there with her. I was in the home stretch when I noticed him take her hand and my heart could've stopped. I literally froze in front of the entire town and had to pull myself together in a hurry."

"I can see that the separation is still very hard on you," Dr. Bryant says. "But you have to know in your soul, I mean, come on, you're a smart guy. You had to know she was eventually going to get back out there."

Dante stares past his computer screen as the words pick at his brain like a healing scab. "I knew this would be a thing, *eventually,*" Dante's knee bounces uncontrollably. "I guess I just expected *eventually* to be when we were in different places in life maybe. It all feels so close, ya know? ... Soon."

"I see," Dr. Bryant spins the ring on his finger. "When you say you *thought you would be in different places in life*, what do you mean?"

"Well, if I'm being honest with you, I've only really told my neighbor this, but I have actually been considering a change in careers."

"Really?" he asks with wide eyes. "Forgive my ignorance, but is a pastor something you can just walk away from?"

"I can make sure someone else is in place before I walk away."

"What brought this on? This is quite sudden, is it not?"

"Maybe. It's been on my mind for a while. Ever since my father passed."

"Why not before?"

Dante chuckles. "How much time you got?"

Dr. Bryant smiles. "Well, Pastor Mitchell, I'm paid by the hour so ... lay it on me."

"Alright, well ... I never saw myself doing this my whole life. I actually don't know what I imagined but I know it was in the industry of helping people. Just not like this."

"What is it about what you do that you don't like?"

"I always saw being a pastor as my dad's thing. I was raised in church, watching him command the watchful eyes each weekend. People loved my father. Before he passed away I was just filling in and helping out. When he passed away, suddenly I was the next up. I felt a little stuck. I still do."

"Well, just like you stepped in for your dad, there has to be someone who steps in for you, right?"

"There are some prospects who help out, but I haven't exactly taken anyone under my wing yet so someone from outside might end up coming in."

"Is that a bad thing?"

"It feels selfish if that's how I let it play out."

"You feel like it is selfish, but at what point do you put your desires first?"

Dante stares at Dr. Bryant on his screen for a moment. "To answer your previous question, about what I don't like ... I don't like the operations of the church. It started to be less about the message and the people more about keeping the lights on."

"I can certainly see that being a turn-off."

"Yeah. It can be distracting. I try so hard, I start every day putting my best foot forward and often feel like I'm standing in place, if not falling behind."

"Would you say that business isn't your niche?"

"Probably not. I'd rather do the work, not the numbers."

"Well, what if you tap someone else to utilize those talents?"

"I suppose it has crossed my mind a time or two."

"Maybe it is time to put that idea to action."

"I have Susan, but she is an older woman. She worked with my dad doing a lot of odd tasks. Some administrative stuff."

"Well, maybe start there?"

Dante snickers. "How do I put this kindly … she isn't the brightest bulb."

"A simpleton, huh?"

"Maybe not as much as I make it seem but every time she says *Mister Dante* I go a little crazier and have to suppress it."

Dr. Bryant offers up a hearty laugh. "I know quite well what you mean. I've had my fair share of those in my day."

"Everything that's happened since my dad passed, Grace leaving, everything with the church … it's just become a lot."

"It sounds like you're stretched a little bit thin, maybe also people-pleasing a bit much, yeah?"

"I spend so much time trying to do good, day to day, so when I let someone down, it bothers me. I just wonder if moving in a direction where I'm not on a stage weekly giving counsel might be more fulfilling to me on a deeper level."

"Dante, I'm going to offer you a bit of validation here today. Your feelings and what you want out of your life are completely valid. It is fair that you see something different for yourself and it's okay if some people are a little miffed by that. You'll *never* be able to please everyone."

"Thanks doc. I feel better hearing that. I haven't told anyone all of that and for you to not treat me like I'm Looney Tunes is a mercy I think I needed."

"A mercy you deserve, Dante."

"I need to find ways to deal with Karl."

"Jealousy?"

"Yeah ... jealousy."

"Well, she is dating, have you considered maybe if you dated you might not be as focused or distracted by her?"

"The thought has crossed my mind but I don't want to hear the town whispering that the pastor's marriage fell apart and then think I can't help them. Plus it feels unfair to subject another woman to that sort of attention."

"So back to people-pleasing?"

Dante's cheek raises with his side smirk. "Touché."

"What do you think people say when they see *her* parading the new fella around? Do you think they've villainized her for dating someone new?"

Dante simmers in the question. "Mason and him, I saw them Sunday, they already have a special freakin' handshake, can you believe that?"

"Kids are imaginative, what's wrong with the handshake?"

Dante rocks his face into his hands and rubs. A sigh expels. "I felt myself getting angry, doc. I think a part of me resents my son a little, maybe."

"I think the perspective here is going to be the key. You're too close to this situation. Remember, Mason is a young boy. A handshake is just a silly little thing kids do. They do it on playgrounds. Lunchrooms. Gymnasiums. It is just a sign of friendship. Endearment. You want your son to be friends and to actually like the person Grace winds up with, right?"

"As opposed to not liking him, of course."

"I think you should consider your son's point of view when it comes to Karl and be mindful of his well-being in addition to your feelings. This is something that being angry or jealous about won't change. You just have to accept it and find the best way for you to move past it."

"I know it seems obvious. But I think you're right."

"You've got a lot going on. Stress is beating you down, but you have got to get up and dodge a few of those punches when you can, do you know what I am trying to say?"

"I think I do."

Dr. Bryant stares at a spiral notepad barely visible on the screen. "Are you still doing the meditations? How are those helping?"

"I do them numerous times a day. They help to center me, just like you said. I find it effective."

"Alright. Love to hear that." His eyes scour the notepad a moment longer. "And are you still taking the medication?"

Dante nods his head. "So far, so good."

"Good, continue taking it," Dr. Bryant urges. "And continue with the breathing and meditating, sounds like it is doing wonders for you."

Dante nods while Dr. Bryant is typing on his end. "You got it."

"Alrighty, so do we want to shoot for the same time next week? Two weeks?"

"Let's go two weeks out."

"Sounds good, Dante. I'll get you scheduled and look out for that confirmation. I'll see ya then."

The meeting ends and the day begins.

CHAPTER EIGHT

FRIDAY

The smell of caramel popcorn and grilled hot dogs permeates the air at the local park as Mason is playing in a little league game. Dante stands behind the fence looking over the umpire's shoulder, cheering on each kid as they come up to bat or play defense. He is the epitome of audibly and visibly supportive. Mason is in the on-deck circle, drawing in the dirt with the head of his bat while he waits for his turn.

"Mason! You got this!" Grace shouts from the stands, across the field from where Dante leans against the fence.

Karl is next to Grace in the crowd among other parents. Dante sees this and thinks of it as a betrayal on a primal level that he cannot explain. *It's bad enough I have to see him on Sundays.*

The kid at the plate strikes out swinging, missing the ball by a foot as the umpire pumps a fist in the air and shouts, "Strrrrrike three!"

Cheers from the visiting bleacher rain onto the field as Mason heads to the plate as his teammate passes him on his way back to the dugout. He digs his cleats into the dirt like the pros do on TV, settling into the batter's box, adjusting his oversized helmet as he readies himself with the bat wagging and his eyes trained on the pitcher.

Dante begins clapping and the other parents join the rally. "Come on, Mason! Let's get this hit, buddy!"

The opposing pitcher is a skinny kid with a nasty fastball for an assumed ten-year-old. The first pitch blows past Mason's bat before he can even react.

"Strike one!" the umpire shouts.

The crowds for both teams cheer loudly for the pitcher and the opposing batter. Mason seems undeterred by the noise. He is locked in and focused. The heel of his front foot is already in motion, ready to explode in an instant, as he waits for the next pitch.

The wind-up.

The pitch.

Mason swings, the whoosh of the composite bat connects with the ball emanating the most satisfying sound followed by uproar and cheer. Mason is at first base before the ball hits the outfield so he keeps running. The ball lands and two of the outfielders get to it quickly. As Mason rolls the dice and goes for third base, a bolt of lightning on his feet, the third baseman stands on the bag waiting for the throw.

Mason slides, the ball smacks the mit as the dirt plumes into a cloud of excitement and labored breathing as he waits for the call.

The umpire throws a punch into the air. "Out!" he yells.

Half of the crowd falls into a series of *awws* while the other half cheers louder at the play. Mason stands and dusts himself off, he kicks at the ground and the other team is coming off of the field. As he comes back to the dugout he slings his helmet against the chain-link fence and it bounces. He takes a seat with his arms crossed and a fire in his face.

Dante claps. "It's alright buddy. Nice hustle. Just keep grinding."

"I was safe!" Mason replies, with venom in his words, nostrils flaring.

"Son, you're gonna have to get over it quickly," Dante tells him through the chain-link fence. "Aren't you pitching?"

Mason ignores the question, arms still crossed, slouching against the wall behind the bench. His other teammates have all gathered their gloves and hats and are sprinting back out to the field.

"Come on son, let's get back out there. There's still a game to play," he says to Mason, who stews a moment longer, with a rage in his eyes that would be enough to scorch the wooden bench. "You know, the best revenge would be striking 'em all out."

Teammates take their positions on the field and are all waiting for him to come out. "Come on, Mason!" someone shouts from shortstop.

"Don't let one bad play ruin it for your team," Dante says with a positivity that is only annoying to Mason at the moment. "Let's get back after it. Go be a team player."

More of his teammates are calling out for him now as he stares onto the field.

The coach walks over. "Everything good here?" he asks. "Mason, if you don't want to pitch we can–"

Mason shoots to his feet and snatches his glove and jogs out to the pitching rubber.

"I think he is just upset about that last call," Dante says to the coach.

"It was a darn good hustle, can't get every close call though," the coach replies.

The change in attitude from Mason over the play has Dante's attention, and even the coach. Mason is normally a mild-mannered kid so an outburst like this is unusual.

Mason stands in the middle of the diamond as the batter steps in, a bigger kid. Mason calls for the ball and makes fast work of his opponent. The kid gets a piece of the first pitch and the ball rolls to the second baseman who throws out the runner at first.

"One out!" the umpire shouts.

The clapping is louder, and Mason is a ball of fire with a face of stone as the next batter comes to the plate. As he brings himself to pitch, he realizes the kid with the bat is their third baseman.

The third baseman who tagged him out.

Mason's cheek tugs at his mouth like a marionette string being pulled by a phantom hand with a malevolent intent, as a smirk is paired with a scowl.

Ready.

Set.

Pitch.

The ball fires from his hand like a rocket propelled grenade and the batter jumps back to avoid taking a fastball to the helmet. A stumble follows and the kid is on his butt in the dirt.

Some choice words and boos spill onto the field as the kid gets back up and steps back into the batter's box.

"Throw it over the plate, kid!" one of the parents shouts.

Mason locks in for the second pitch. Up and inside, the batter tenses up and the ball sinks right into his ribs. The bat drops, and with the wind knocked out of him he crashes to the dirt, hunched over as the umpire checks on him. The other team's coach rushes out to check on his athlete. Mason stands there, glove raised, calling for the ball with no reaction to what just happened.

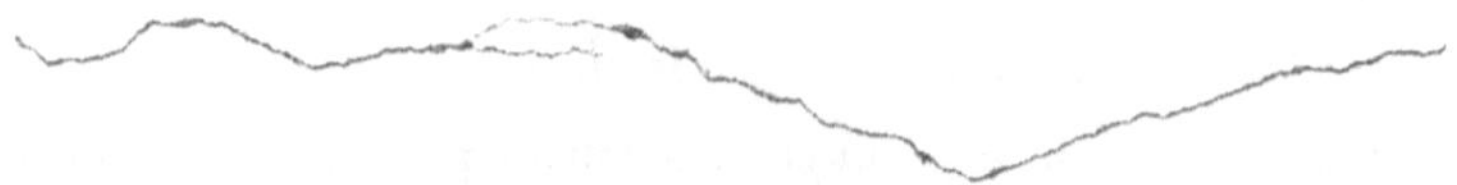

After the game, Dante and Mason are in the car, heading home. Only the sound of the road moving beneath them fills the car. That is until Dante turns on the radio. *Livin' on a Prayer* by Bon Jovi plays at a low volume. Mason stares ahead, not offering much in ways of conversation.

Dante can't help himself from glancing over at Mason every few seconds. Like a parent desperate for connection, "So," he starts. "What was that out there today?"

No words are spoken back, only the sound of oncoming traffic whipping past the car, and the dull harmony of the music playing.

"You know, you could have really hurt that kid today."

Mason flares his nostrils.

That's more of a response than silence, Dante thinks.

"I was safe."

Dante lets the words marinate for a second, seeking a thoughtful response. "Well, safe or not ... there were better ways for you to have handled yourself out there today."

Mason stares ahead as they are stopped at a red light. Feeling his father's eyes on him, he shrugs.

"What do you mean," Dante shrugs back, "what if it were you that took a pitch to the ribs?"

Mason rolls his eyes.

"Don't roll your eyes at me, son. I'm being serious here. This is not okay for you to be acting this way." The light turns green and Dante lets his foot off the brake. "And you shouldn't be talking this way to me. I am your father. You need to show me respect. I know you know better too."

"I don't care."

"You don't care!?" Dante asks, shocked. "Well, maybe a nice time-out with no games will be good for you."

Mason bolts upright, turning to his dad. "The hell?"

Dante's eyes go wide, turning to Mason, "Mason! Language!"

"Why am I in trouble?"

"How are you not understanding why you *are* in trouble?"

"I was right, they were wrong, and now I'm being punished," Mason leans back hard, crossing his arms.

Dante keeps his eyes on the road as he keeps the car moving while allowing the tension in the front seat to disband. "I just wish you would have at least apologized to that kid. We raised you better than that."

"I wish I would've thrown it harder," Mason says through clenched teeth and flaring nostrils.

Mason's attitude commands that Dante look at him, but words are hard to come by. "Maybe we'll just talk about this later," Dante turns up the music a few notches, "when you've cooled off."

Chapter Nine

As Dante and Mason come through the front door, they are greeted with a wall of steamy fog. Dante is alarmed and takes careful steps inside waving his hand through the thick fog in the living room. The sound of the kitchen sink faucet running fills the space and Dante cautions himself, tapping the sink handle before turning it off. The heat radiates from the handle as the steam it produces starts to settle.

He studies the sink counter and surrounding areas to see moisture on the surface of pretty much everything. He leans against the lip of the sink, palms pressed firm, as he can't hold back a short paradoxical laugh.

Mason stands in the living room, staring at his father. "What happened?"

Dante turns to look at his son from over his shoulder. "You left the water running before we left is what happened."

Mason's eyes shift. "But I didn't use the kitchen sink this morning."

"Okay," Dante turns around, leans his back against the counter and crosses his arms. "Well I know for a fact I would not have left the hot water running, full pressure at that." His eyes rip through his son, who suddenly seems smaller as he stands there.

"I didn't do that!"

"Only two of us were in this house this morning," Dante says, raising his voice as he steps toward his son. "And I know that I didn't do it, so just fess up!"

"I don't know why you're blaming me!" Mason shouts, his voice nearly screeching. "I told you I didn't do it!" He turns away from his father and marches up the stairs, each foot falling harder than the last. "And I don't know why you won't believe me!" he shouts, his voice tearing through the house right before he slams the bedroom door to put an exclamation mark on the accusation as the walls rattle.

As Dante allows some time for cooler heads to prevail, he straightens up the house. As he takes out the trash, he is greeted by Barry and a few of his police buddies. The men huddle around the grill, all with a bottle or can of some kind in hand.

"Howdy, neighbor!" Barry greets, raising a pair of tongs as he takes a sip.

"Good afternoon, Barry," Dante says, and then looking at the men around him, "and gentlemen," he nods.

The others all give nods and exchange salutations as Dante tosses the bag into a can and lets the lid slam shut.

"Dante, this is Dennis." Dennis raises a bottle. "This is Clay." Clay smirks and winks. "And this young buck over here is Boyd." Boyd's all-white beard and tired body suggest he was anything but young.

Dante leans against the fence. "Nice to meet you, fellas. I'm Dante, Dante Mitchell."

Boyd perks up, "The pastor," he asks, with a cigarette bouncing on his lips, "down at Heart of Our Savior?"

Dante smiles, nodding, "Yep, that would be the one."

"Dante's a good guy, good neighbor, even if he takes Jesus over football," Barry razzes, laughing at his own joke. His friends all laugh along in light-spirited jollies.

"My wife and her friends go to your church Dante," Clay says. "They really seem to like it. Sounds like you do a good job there."

"Well thank you, that's great to hear."

"I used to attend years back," Boyd says. "Another pastor, older fella, used to run the show."

Dante nods along. "That was probably my father."

"Oh, Jesus, I don't recall how long ago that might have been but, well I'd say it's been at least a decade," Boyd says. "How is the old man?"

Reluctant to answer, Dante finds himself navigating the conversation he seems to have had a thousand times now in a short time. "He actually passed away a little over a year ago."

"Way to go, Boyd," Dennis interjects.

"Shit," Boyd replies. "I'm sorry to hear that. I didn't mean to–"

"It's okay," Dante assures. "It is something that I've talked about a bit now and since taking over his position I've had to answer to plenty of folks with lots of concerns. Don't worry yourself."

Barry opens the clamshell to the grill and the smoke plumes out. "So what's going on, Holy man? You look a little stressed. Want a beer?" Barry asks with a childish grin, already knowing the answer.

Dante laughs as an answer of its own before letting out a sigh. "It's just Mason."

"He's gettin' to be that age," Barry says, flipping burger patties attentively.

"How old is ya boy?" Clay asks.

"Ten."

"He givin' you a lot of lip?" Dennis asks.

"Actually, yeah," Dante replies. "All of a sudden this kid is a wildfire."

"You know, back in my day, my pops would've busted me in the mouth if I talked back," Boyd says.

"This ain't the eighteen-hundreds old man. You can't tell a pastor to hit his kid anyhow. You're a cop, you should know better."

Boyd groans as he ambles over to the picnic bench. "Agh, toe-may-toe, toe-motto."

Dennis and Clay stand with plates in hand, laughing at the grumpy old man they work with. Barry tosses some buns onto their plates as he suggests to Dante, "You ever thought about putting Mason in karate or soccer? Something more physical maybe. Help him get some of that energy out."

Dante watches him serve up the meats, less burnt than last time. "He's playing baseball right now and it is challenging enough to work that out between his mother and me, and trying to work."

"Baseball is good … it's not football, but it's good."

"He had an incident on the field this morning. Led to me giving him a firm talkin' to."

"Want one?" Barry asks, offering a burger to Dante.

"Sure," Dante responds.

Barry prepares a plate with a bun and gathers the condiments. "What happened this morning? He chase after some kid with a bat or somethin'?"

Dante takes the plate from Barry from over the fence. "Thank you."

"No problem," Barry replies.

"No, no bat, but close. He pitched a kid up and in, then put one in his ribs for tagging him out at third, the inning before. The other kid went down like a bag of hammers."

"Holy shit!" Clay lets out.

"Watch your fuckin' mouth Clay!" Boyd commands.

"Ope, sorry Dante."

Dante laughs. "It's alright." He takes a big bite out of the sandwich.

Barry stares at Dante, eyes peeled open as he shakes his head. "Little Mason, my little buddy, he did that?"

"Yep," Dante answers with a mouthful. "I'm just as put off by it as you, believe me."

"Might be time for you to have a more direct talk about consequences and respect," Barry suggests.

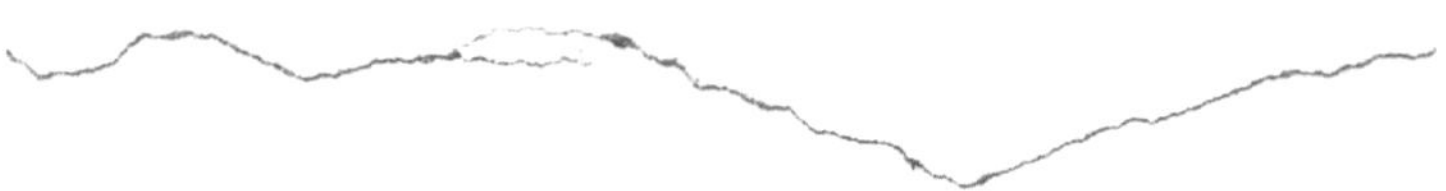

Dante is on the phone with Grace, touching base on what happened today at the game. They've been bickering on the phone for over ten minutes already.

"Yes, I tried to talk to him on the drive home. He didn't have much to say. He's still angry about–"

"Then you said he came home and was slamming doors too? And cursing? That just isn't like him," Grace cuts in.

"The hot water in the kitchen sink had been running all morning. I'm positive he left it on before we left," Dante adds.

The silence hangs on the line between them for a moment. *"Are you sure you don't want me to come get him? It sounds like–"*

Dante interrupts, "No, it's fine. We just need to cool off. Both of us got hot. He is getting older and I think maybe it's hormones or something."

"Are you sure? Offer stands if you decide you want the night to yourself."

"Grace, I can take care of my son. One little spat isn't going to make me want to send him packing. Jeez."

"*I'm not– That isn't what I was trying to say.*" Dante allows her the space to explain but the extended pause is evident that the conversation has nowhere productive left to go, only to make things more uncomfortable for them both.

"I'm gonna get off here ... listen, everything is fine. I will try talking to him. It will be fine."

Grace hesitates, surrendering a sigh. "*Okay.*"

"Okay ... goodnight Grace. I will talk to you tomorrow."

"*Goodnight.*"

They hang up and Dante is ready to wind down for the evening. He takes the phone to his bedside and puts it on the charger before heading back downstairs to finish cleaning up around the house. As he tries to decompress, his nervous energy has him wiping things he has already wiped, and shuffling things around the countertops that don't need to be moved. As he's hyper-focusing on things in the house, his eyes fall hard onto a photo on the wall. It's a framed photo from when they had their pictures taken at a studio a few years back.

The three of them.

When they were together.

When they were happy.

He stares at a version of himself that wears a smile, hiding a man that doesn't know how bad he is hurting his family. Grace stands close to him, as beautiful and loving as ever, portraying herself as a woman who isn't already broken.

Not yet, anyway.

Her smile only suppresses the feelings she has, and how trapped she must feel. Dante hangs his head for a moment. Hindsight is a useless tool when it comes to reflecting on what went wrong and he recognizes how much of a facade this picture really is. The only genuine thing is Mason. Under his mother's arm, smiling into the camera with a cheesy grin that tells the camera that his innocence is still intact.

That smile ... something about it isn't right. The longer Dante looks at the photo, the blurrier Mason's face becomes. He looks away to adjust his eyes and as he takes another glance, Mason's portrait looks like it's been smeared. Like a wet smudge over his face. *Must've been from the hot water earlier. Strange that it is only Mason's face though,* he thinks to himself.

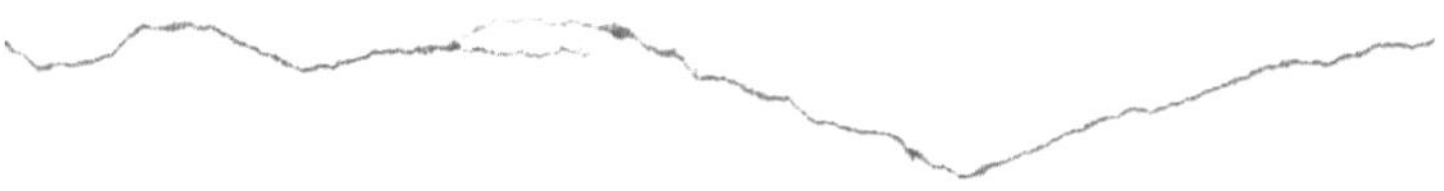

Dante heads upstairs, knocking on Mason's door as he enters. "Hey pal," he says. Mason lies there in silence and looks away as his father takes a seat at the foot of the bed. "I get it. I messed up today. I just wanted to apologize to you, for earlier. You told me you didn't leave the water on and I probably should believe you more. Lord knows I would want the same from my father when I was your age." Dante rests his hand on Mason's shoulder and watches him lay there. "Alright, I'll leave you to it. I love you, son," he says as he gets up. "Goodnight." He pulls the door shut and makes his way back downstairs.

CHAPTER TEN

D ante drags his tired body downstairs and into the dining room where the computer awaits. He opens the laptop and signs on and heads to Youtube to record a video. He tousles his hair and yawns before he presses the *record* button. He sits for a moment considering what he might say that could be meaningful and different from anything he has said before, or at best, recently.

"Good evening friends, neighbors, brothers, sisters." He leans back in his office chair and taps on the desk while staring out of frame. The thoughts are heavy where words are lacking. He looks at the screen and sees he has been recording for nearly a minute. "You know, today was an exhausting one. I'm not too naive to think that every day is going to be the best. If it were, then we'd all be havin' *best days* and you know what that would mean?" Dante sits upright and leans closer to the camera. "It means we wouldn't need to rely on God. He gives us challenges. He tests our faith to draw us closer to Him. God never promised we wouldn't face hardships, but He is there, at our side, along every step of our journey. God is going to test you. He is going to challenge you. He is going to shape your iron with those bad days, and you know what? That's okay. Because there will come a time when you are soaring high again, and those right there, those are the times where God rewards you for staying true to your faith when the days were hard ... hug your family just a little tighter on these days, you'll need them when the days aren't going well. I'm not exempt from God's challenges, but I made it through and I know you can too. Please, take a moment, and join me in prayer now."

Dante recites a prayer and promptly stops the recording and uploads it to Youtube. He takes a moment to share the link on the church's Facebook page and he shuts the computer for the evening.

All cleaned up and even making time to meditate, Dante is deep into his nightly routine. Lying in his cool bed, he lets his thoughts drift and his eyelids flutter as the much welcomed grip of a peaceful night's sleep takes him away. The silence in the room becomes a muddy sound that becomes tangled with his passive thoughts. Mason's recent attitude, before the hot water, before the fastball to the kid's ribs, before the raised voice at the dinner table. The replay of the day is so vivid to him while he slips into dreamland. He and Mason are back in the car driving and they're both back in the conversation about the baseball game that morning.

"I just wish you would have apologized."

"I wish I would've thrown it harder," Mason says, not breaking his fixed stare ahead.

Dante is unable to hide the shock from that statement. The intent of harming someone is concerning. "Son, you know better. You can't just–"

"But I was safe, dad!" Mason interrupts. "I was safe!" Mason's voice grows in volume. "Safe!" his voice multiplies with each word, as he turns in his seat and stares through his dad. "Safe! Safe! Safe!"

Dante looks at his son in horror, not only at his negative demeanor, but his face has gone pale, his eyes glassy and black with splintering veins crawling away from his eyes just beneath his skin as he continues to speak. Suddenly it's not a sunny afternoon drive, but night has fallen and oncoming headlights pass only showing the most terrifying parts of Mason's face as he continues.

"Safe! Safe! Safe! Safe!"

"Mason! Knock it off already! What are–"

"Safe! Safe! Safe! *Dafe*! Dad! Dad! Dad!"

Dante jolts from his sleep, heart racing despite his stillness.

"Dad!"

Dante leaps to the floor and races to Mason's bedroom. Not bothering to knock, he bursts in not being quiet at all. Breathing heavily he stands in the doorway watching his son, sound asleep.

What a messed up dream, he thinks. Certain that he heard Mason calling for him, the confusion wears on him. He goes to the bathroom and has a drink of water from the sink. Staring at the tired-eyed reflection in the mirror, he accepts that he has had an emotional day, and has been a little stressed lately and maybe that was just an outlier as far as vivid dreams are concerned. Although, *nightmare* may be more accurate. Dante decides to quietly return to bed and hopes that he can get some sleep without the strange dreams.

He slides back into bed and it engulfs him into a warm and inviting place of slumber. Just as he is stretched out and falling asleep though, there is noise coming from downstairs. The TV is on, maybe. Dante raises up, groaning. He walks out of his room and recognizes that it isn't just the TV. It's music. A familiar song. *Livin' on a Prayer* has been in his head all day since hearing it in the car earlier. The hair on his arms and neck raise and he rushes down to turn it off. He gets into the living room and Spotify is on the TV and the volume is higher than it ever is any other day. He turns off the TV as fast as he grabs the remote and that is when he hears the unmistakable sound of the ceiling fan in the dining room.

The fan is on high and the blades whip and whirl so fast that the stem is moving in a stirring motion like it might tear itself from the ceiling. The pull chains rattle against the light globe and Dante is quick to stop the fan. Silence fills the home and he stands in his dining room completely befuddled. He doesn't wait long to go back upstairs, checking on Mason on his way. Mason repositions in his bed as the door opens.

"Goodnight, Mason," Dante's whisper carries. "I love you." Dante goes to his bedroom and falls into bed and lets the mattress swallow him up. He lies restless for a while as he ponders on what is happening in his home. Not just that the TV turned on, or that the ceiling fan was on a speed that he never uses, but the song specifically leaves an unsettling feeling in his gut, along with the catchy earworm that is played by that band. He doesn't watch horror movies but he has heard and seen enough to understand that is something that only happens in those late night flicks he was always told not to watch as a kid. As he does the mental gymnastics that tire him out, he eventually drifts off into sleep.

CHAPTER ELEVEN

SATURDAY

It's Saturday morning and the summertime sun creeps through the blinds, warming Dante's face. He looks at the time and sits up, hanging his feet off of the side of the bed. He wipes his eyes and rests his hands on the edge of the mattress, yawning with a morning roar that unhinges his jaw before he gets on his feet. With his eyes pulled tight and his maw wide, he lets out an involuntary sound. As his eyes open, he gets up and opens the blinds, allowing the sunlight to pour in. He watches outside as one of the neighbors is being dragged from the leash and pulled out of their shoes by their eager dog.

His eyes adjust to the reflection in the window glass and he sees an unfocused blur behind him. As he looks closer, he sees that it's more like a shadow. It looms in the doorway and his blood chills at the sight. Unwilling to take his eyes off of the figure, he feels wide awake. It's like the two are having a staredown, only just as he commits to watching the shadow blur, it moves.

He turns on his heels quickly to find Mason in his room walking toward him. "Dad, can we have pancakes, please?"

Dante's heart thuds in his chest as the air is trapped in his throat. "Sheesh!" he says, gripping his chest, frozen in place. He catches his breath while Mason waits there. "Sure, buddy. Why don't you go downstairs and I'll be down there in a minute."

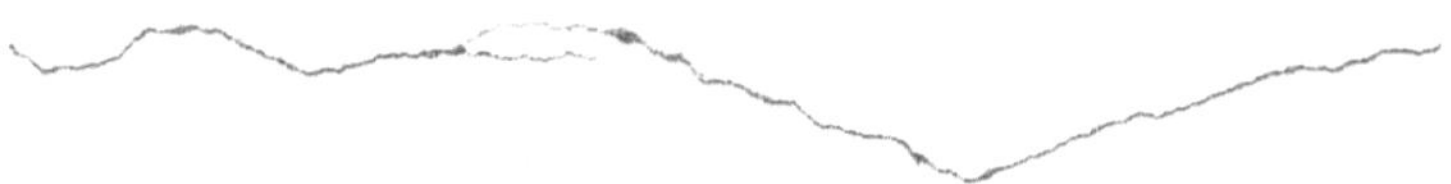

Mason sits at the counter on a barstool while Dante is making pancakes. "Can you make mine shaped like a dog?"

"Sure!" Dante says, enthusiastically. He's happy to be exchanging words this morning. A good night of sleep seems to have done well for the two of them.

"Can you make it look like Karl's dog, Votto?"

Dante drops the spatula at the mention of Karl. Scrambling to collect himself, he retrieves it. "Sure," he says. "Is he a big or small dog?"

Mason twists his face with a look of thoughtfulness. "Um, medium, I think."

Dante can't help but to roll his eyes. "You got it," he says. *What kind of person names a dog after a baseball player?* he wonders, letting the ugly judgmental thoughts creep in and take the stage.

Breakfast is served and Dante slides onto a stool beside Mason at the counter. Mason has a short stack that he pours an obnoxious amount of syrup on. "You want some pancakes to go with your syrup, kid?" Dante jokes as he has already begun eating. "I'm glad to see you're in a much better mood today, son."

"Mhm," Mason nods, squeezing a little more syrup onto his maple-soaked stack.

"So," Dante starts. "What do you wanna get into today? It's a beautiful day out."

Mason picks up a box of herbal tea that is on the counter and is studying the packaging. "I don't know. I was–" Mason goes silent with his attention fixed on the small tea packaging.

"Hey, you okay, bud?" Dante places a hand on Mason's shoulder and gets no reaction. Mason sits, transfixed in space from a barstool. "Hey!" Dante jars him, this time with urgency in his voice. "Mason."

Mason's attention snaps back to earth with confusion painted on his face. "What!?"

"You spaced out for a sec there," Dante replies. "How come you didn't answer me?"

"What did you say?"

Dante stares at him, enamored by whatever that was. Dante is feeling uneasy about his son these last few days. "Nothing. Eat your breakfast."

Mason begins digging the side of his fork into his stack of pancakes and loads up for a big bite. He is still studying the packaging of tea with fascination. With a mouthful of food he begins reading the directions aloud. "Bring fresh water to a boil. Pour water into cup. Add teabag and let it brew."

Dante continues eating his breakfast as Mason repeats the directions.

"Bring fresh water to a boil. Pour water into cup. Add teabag and let it brew."

"You're really into tea all of a sudden, aren't ya?" Dante jeers.

Mason repeats, progressively louder each time. "Bring fresh water to a boil. Pour water into cup. Add teabag and let it brew."

Dante sets his fork down. "Alright, that's enough now. Why don't we just calm down about the tea."

"Bring fresh water to a boil. Bring fresh water to a boil. Bring fresh water to a boil!" He is practically screaming. "Bring fresh water to a boil! Bring fresh water to a–"

Mason freezes. "Mason!" Dante grabs his shoulders and shakes him. Silence lingers between them as Mason blinks. Dante's sigh of relief is one of many in a short span of time.

Mason looks around the house, then down at his pancakes. His body language makes him seem out of place.

Lost.

"You okay?"

"Can we go ride bikes later?" he asks, clueless as to anything unusual happening.

With apprehension, Dante studies Mason's face and his mannerisms. Something is clearly off about his son and every alarm in his head is sounding off as red flags are raised. "Sure. Finish your food and help me clean up though."

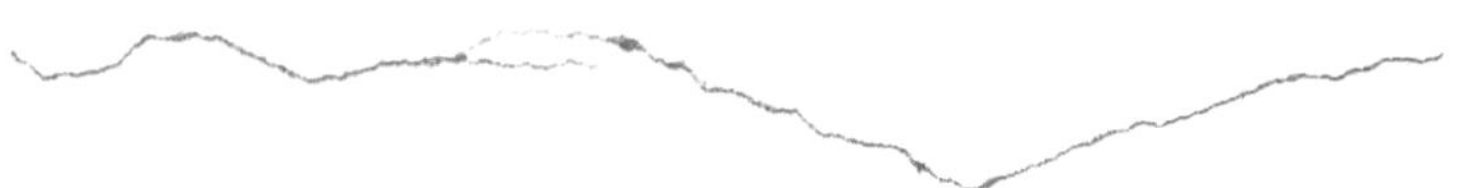

The men of the house are at a nearby park. Dante is walking along while Mason pedals his Huffy up and down the walkway while Dante is on the phone with Grace.

He is getting older. Maybe this is just puberty or something, Grace suggests.

"I don't know," Dante says with reluctance. "You weren't there. It was weird. Things have been strange the last few days. The thing with the water, the TV, the ceiling fan. Then the ..." Dante lowers his voice to ensure Mason isn't able to hear, "creepy little breakfast episode. I'm really worried about him."

Grace sighs. *Well ... he had that baseball game. Do you think maybe he got a concussion or something?*

"I don't think so," Dante dismisses. "There wasn't any hard contact. Besides, you'd likely see signs of a concussion sooner. I don't think that's it."

Mason whips past Dante going dangerously fast. "Dad!" he shouts. "Look how fast I'm going!" Mason raises his behind off the seat to go even faster. "Weeeeee!"

"That's awesome buddy," Dante hollers. "Why don't you slow down a little?"

Do you think it's worth getting looked at anyway? Grace asks.

"I don't know. Seems like a waste of time and a co-pay."

Don't you think we should, just to be sure?

"I just don't think that's what's going on."

Okay ... what do you think is going on then? Grace prods.

Mason comes speeding by again, pedalling his legs as hard as they can possibly go when suddenly the chain on the bike pops. The crank and pedals go spinning wildly and Mason squeezes the hand brake and skids on his feet to stop. "Aw, crap!"

"Mason! Language!" Dante says, sternly.

"I didn't say anything! I said crap!"

"I gotta go. Mason just popped his chain. Catch up later?" Dante asks.

Yeah. Call me later, Grace says before hanging up.

Mason stands beside his bike as it lies on the sidewalk. Dante approaches it with a smirk. "Just going a little too fast, kiddo. Let me have a look."

Before Dante can get over to the bike, Mason has already flipped it upside down, resting it on the seat and handlebars with the wheels pointing to the sky. "It's okay, I got it."

"You know what you're doing, son?" Dante asks, voice laced with doubt.

"Mhm," Mason responds as he grabs hold of the greasy chain and guides it onto the crank. "Karl showed me how to fix it."

Karl.

Dante feels his face heating up and his blood thumping throughout his body. "Of course he did," he says, like a whisper sneaking away from his tongue, unable to filter himself.

He feels a buzzing in his pocket and sees Susan is calling him. "Hey, Susan. How are you?"

I'm good, Mister Dante. I was just calling to see if you needed me to pick up some plasticware for the luncheon tomorrow.

"Have you checked the kitchen pantry? If we don't have any we can ask Richie over at Costco about donating some items."

I'm at Walmart now and can go ahead and—

"No, no, no, Susan. I will take care of it today. Don't worry about it."

Are you sure? If everyone shows up who normally attends tomorrow we aren't going to have enough.

"I appreciate your concern. I will take care of it today."

Susan pauses. *Okay,*

"I'll see you tomorrow morning."

Sure will. God bless.

He hangs up and cannot help but smile as he watches his son, already having the bike tires back on the ground and rolling. Despite the mixed feelings of another man teaching his son, he still beams with pride.

Chapter Twelve

The two return home after a hot afternoon at the park. Mason leaves his bike on the porch with intentions to put it away later, which isn't an unusual thing for him to do. Dante shuffles the keys into the door to go inside and upon entry he is hit with concern. His nostrils flare, picking up scents of warmth, like the offensive odor of hot electricity.

"Do you smell that?"

Mason looks around, puts his nose forward and sniffs around. "It smells like something is burning."

Dante tosses the keys into a dish and takes urgent steps through the main floor of the home. He sees no smoke, but as he comes closer to the kitchen hears the buzzing coming from the stove. "What in the world?" The electric burners on the stovetop all glow an ominous orange. He is fast to turn all of the range knobs off and immediately the burners stop glowing. "How did these–" Without processing what happened, he turns to Mason.

Mason stands quietly in the dining room as he watches his father handle it. Dante's eyes lock onto Mason's and the boy looks to the floor.

"Was this you?" Dante asks, taking steps toward his son. Mason avoids eye contact and shuffles his feet backwards. "Do you know how dangerous this is?"

Mason flinches as his father raises his voice. "It wasn't me," he says softly.

"Right, just like the water wasn't you too?" Dante scolds, seething with an eye roll. "Shoot it straight with me, kid. Is this an attention thing? Are you mad at me?"

"It wasn't me!" Mason shouts. His eyes welling up, his voice laced with anger.

"Hey!" Dante bellows, his voice ringing through the house. "Do not raise your voice at me!"

Mason storms off, stomping through the living room, approaching the stairs, he stops and turns to Dante. "I don't know how to talk to you! I told you it wasn't me and you won't believe me!"

Dante stomps through the house toward Mason, who races up the stairs, each foot moving faster than the last. He runs into his bedroom and slams the door. The house shakes as the sound infringes on the silence inside. Dante stops at the bottom of the steps, leaning on the banister as he decides what to do next. The pastor is often showing others how to deal with conflict within families and how to constructively build on relationships. This is an opportunity for him to practice what he preaches, so to speak. Rather than for him to march upstairs and yell some more, he decides that a break might do them both some good.

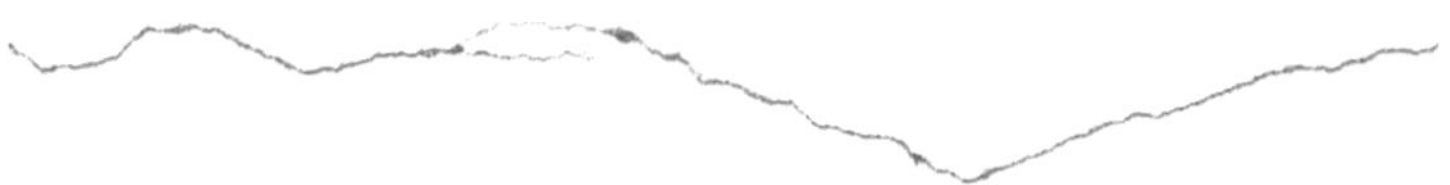

It is well into the evening and very little has been said between the two. Dante hollers up to tell Mason to come eat only for Mason to tell him that he isn't hungry. The wear of single parenting is beginning to show on Dante's face and how he wears his collared button-up shirt untucked, half unbuttoned, sporting wrinkles from throughout the day. After cleaning up and feeling unsettled about leaving things so tense between him and his son, he decides to make another attempt to talk with him.

Dante heads up the stairs and raps his knuckles against the door gently. "Hey, Mason. Can I come in?" Dead air comes from the other side of the door. Dante pauses for a moment with his hand on the knob. "I'm coming in."

When he opens the door, he sees Mason standing at his window, staring out over the backyard with his back to his father.

Dante steps in and leans against the dresser. "You know, I'm not mad at you Mason, you can come eat, and hang out like we normally do. You understand that, right?"

Mason inhales and the sound of his nostrils only offer a contained rage within him.

"Look, I know that I said some things, but don't you think how you're acting is a little bit–"

Mason interjects. "Get ... out."

Dante stands there, stunned, with his hands on his hips as he looks around the room uncertain of how to respond. His instinct is to correct Mason and demand he show him respect, but the more rational voice in his head is urging him to treat Mason more like a person, and less like a child. With it becoming more difficult to not scream at Mason, Dante has the relationship between his son and Karl blurring his vision. Yelling would be easy, but would possibly only drive Mason closer to his mother's new boyfriend.

Mason inhales once more in a way that feels like a lit fuse than a deep breath.

Dante lets out a chortle. "Listen, I'm not leaving until you turn around and talk to me." Dante steps toward Mason. "I understand you're angry, and that's okay but you need to show me some respect."

He places a calm hand on Mason's shoulder only to be shrugged away. "I said to go. I don't want to talk to you," Mason says in a calm, yet threatening voice.

Dante slides his rejected hands into his pockets and stares out the window beside his son. "Well ... if you don't want to talk right now, will you at least tell me what you do want?"

Mason inhales audibly once more. The air in his chest begins to feel like a coiled rattlesnake issuing a warning. He turns to his father, looking up at him. "What do I want?" he asks. "I want to go home. To my *real* home!" he shrieks. Dante's eyes peel open wide. "I want to go be with mom. I want to be with Karl, who doesn't make me do things I don't want to do," he says, venom spewing from his heart. "And most of all, I want to get away from *you*!" he roars, like a final nail driven by the heavy crash of a hammer.

Dante runs his hand through his hair and paces away from Mason. The words rip through him and nearly draw tears. "You know what?" Dante says, rushing toward Mason, getting in his face. "You can be mad all night, you can feel however you want, but you can't say those things to me. Do you even understand how disrespectful and nasty that was to say to me?" Mason steps back, eyebrows lowered and eyes squinting as his nostrils flare. "Do you realize everything I do for you? I've sacrificed to make sure you can have a cushy life in the suburbs? You think I like being away so much? Huh!?" Dante snaps.

Mason takes it all in with no reaction. He has heard this all before when his parents used to argue. Dante's effort to show Mason all of the reasons he should be grateful only pushes him to feel closer to his mother. Mason watches his father begin to pace again, nose scrunching with a smolder in his eyes that could set this house on fire. He takes the opportunity to hop onto his bed after Dante puts a little space between them.

"I make sure you can play sports, I make sure you understand the value of Jesus Christ, our Lord and Savior. I make sure to be a part of your life despite your mother and I–" Dante stops his emotional rant, turning his back to Mason to hide his eyes that have started welling up. Dante feels his voice under the grip of heartache and the flood of tears he is desperately fighting back. The flood of feelings becomes overwhelming. The hurt, the pressure, the need to be attentive to not only the people of his father's congregation, but to be there for his family, or what's left of it. The need to salvage everything dear to him is heavier than ever...and that's when the levee breaks and the tears begin to stream.

Dante turns to face Mason. "I care about you so much, and this is how you treat me. I'm so disappointed in–" Mason lunges at his father from the bed with a deep roar, interrupting him. His body smacks into Dante's chest, knocking him off balance. He drops to the floor as Mason corrects his body to mount his father. He sits on his stomach and punches at his chest. Dante's reflexes takeover and he restrains Mason, grabbing both of his wrists to stop the raining blows.

Mason wriggles away and gets to his feet as Dante shoves him away and jumps to his. The two of them stand off, winded and in defensive positions.

"You need to leave now," Mason says through ragged air, his tone sounding like someone else entirely.

Dante rotates his right arm and feels his shoulder and notices blood. He stares at the crimson color on his fingertips and his eyes lock on to Mason. "What in the world has gotten into you!?" he yells, staring at his son like a stranger with horror on his face, wiping the blood onto his shirt.

Mason sneers at his father as he lowers his head. "I could ask you the same."

Dante burst out of the bedroom, clutching his shoulder. As he gets to the end of the hallway, the door slams behind him, startling him enough to look back. The hallway at his back is dark and something is wrong with Mason. He goes downstairs and is focused on cleaning up the bleeding and wrapping his head around whatever that was that just happened.

His shirt comes off and he hangs it over the right side of the kitchen sink. He grabs a towel and retrieves a first-aid kit from a closet. The wooden legs of the chair scream against the floor as he takes a seat at the dining room table. He works fast, dousing the towel with rubbing alcohol and applying it to his shoulder. He tenses up at the first touch, breathing in loud through his clenched teeth.

The pain only lasts a moment while the antiseptic obliterates any bacteria that could cause infection. Everything upstairs happened so fast, and seemingly for no reason that he could think of. Nothing between them should have led to his ten-year-old son acting so erratic and violent. The injury had to come from falling on something when Mason launched himself at him. Maybe he scraped his shoulder on the molding of the floor. It wasn't worth worrying about how it happened, but more so about what is happening to Mason. The concern has Dante considering his best course of action as the parent. Mason has never acted this way before, and before this week, he was always calm, respectful, and the typical boy who just wants to play.

Dante considers calling Grace, but he feels like he has called and texted her a lot in a span of only a few days, only to gripe about Mason's behavior. He doesn't want to continue bothering her with this, especially since he is the parent too and more than capable of taking care of his son.

As he pats his wound dry and prepares to bandage it up, his glance catches the framed photo from before, still sitting on the table. He stops what he is doing and reaches for the photo to inspect it. Mason's face is even more warped and deteriorated than before and now he is noticing his own face in the family photo. Holding the frame closer to his face, he sees himself in the photograph, facial features nearly unrecognizable. Blurred and oversaturated like watercolor paints with too much moisture. He shakes his head and lays the photo back down on the table. It must have been residual water from the other day when the sink was left running.

Once he tidies up his wound and gets his bandage on he allows himself time to meditate. Dr. Bryant has been adamant that he makes the time to meditate, and considering the events that have unfolded recently, it seems more critical now than ever that he center himself and come back calm and level-headed. He takes his meds and guzzles a glass of water over the sink before heading upstairs to his bedroom.

Chapter Thirteen

With eyes sealed tight, air flows freely as his chest rises and falls, all while planted comfortably on a pillow on the floor, Dante embraces the moment to get focused. The energy in the home is sour ... the tension is thick. Every word exchanged is laced with needles and every cut seems to strike a nerve. Tiny emotional bombs are left in Dante's mind nearly every time that Mason speaks and this situation is unlike anything he has faced, let alone counseled, ever.

His mind wanders, only moments removed from what happened in Mason's room, proving difficult to focus on the breathing. Dante tries anyway. He inhales deep through his nose, his thoughts find their way to Mason's expression. He had never looked at his father that way. The notion of Mason hating him was terrifying and even more heartbreaking. He exhales through his mouth in a long release.

Let the thoughts go. Focus on the breathing.

He inhales deep, drawing air through his nose in a massive gulp. His thoughts reach for other burdens. Through his stream of consciousness, he latches onto the sight of Grace holding hands with Karl in the church. With his cheeks flushed, he is aware of his heart pounding harder in his chest. His blood forcing through his veins at a velocity that would concern the average physician. Mason's constant praise and adoration for Karl only fuels the palpable anger. He exhales through his mouth once more in a long, slow release.

Let the thoughts go. Focus on the breathing.

Another deep breath fills his lungs. The sudden vision of Mason standing in a field as it burns around him fills his reverie. His son stands with his back to him, unbothered by the flames that dance around him, close enough to sear his flesh, but paying no mind to the threat of burning no matter how smothering the heat feels against his skin. Dante's heart begins to race more and he releases the breath sooner than he should as he tries to shake this dark thought.

Let the thoughts go. Focus on the breathing.

He inhales deep, once more. Recognizing the stir of thoughts and events weighing heavy in his heart, he pivots to counting, just like Dr. Bryant taught him. He holds his breath for five seconds and counts in his head before releasing. He's careful to make sure his release is longer than that as well. This repeats until the anger fades and the sense of calm is there. As he lets out a yawn, he thinks that now would be a good time to stop.

With a clear mind, he's ready to confront his son and make things right, no matter what it might take. About forty-five minutes have passed since Mason's attack and Dante hopes this is enough time for Mason to have reflected on his own actions. Dante paces down the hallway and hovers outside of the door, hesitating, as he hasn't thought out what to say. *Best to speak from the heart and focus on keeping the interaction calm,* he thinks. With a knock on the door he waits for a response to be met with silence, as expected at this point.

"Hey kiddo," he says as he opens the door and pokes his head in. Mason is sitting in the dark on his bed. His legs criss-cross apple-sauce, just like they teach in elementary school.

Dante is put off by the sight as he notices his son staring straight ahead and mumbling to himself, not acknowledging Dante's presence whatsoever. "Can we talk, son?" Dante opens the door wide as the light from the hallway spills in, lighting up the room as he steps inside. "I'd really like to talk, you know, make things right with us." Mason's eyes stay fixed on what's in front of him, less like he is looking at anything, but more like he is spaced out. His mumbling continues. "Mason, are you even listening to me?" he asks, grabbing his son's shoulder and nudging him.

Mason's eyes remain glazed over but his mumbling becomes a more coherent babble. "Bring fresh water to a boil, bring fresh water to a boil, bring fresh water to a boil," he repeats aloud. The same as before with breakfast.

Dante nudges him again, "What are you going on about with the tea?" he asks. The chanting stops. Mason closes his eyes and his head turns to his father, slowly. Dante staggers backwards at the change of Mason's eyes as they open and peer into him. Mason's eyes give off a blue-ish gray hue, similar to shark skin, accompanied with a smile that stretches across his face. He blinks once more to reveal obsidian black eyes, smooth as glass, and deep as space.

Mason unfolds his legs and his movement explodes, startling Dante, as he backs out into the hallway with fear clutching words that won't seem to escape his throat. He is a spectator to the show his son is putting on. The balls of Mason's feet dig into the mattress and propel him backwards, putting him in an unnatural position with his back arching in an exaggerated way. His movements are jerky and he contorts his limbs as his joints audibly crack and snap. With his body tensing up, and muscles and tendons outstretched and at their limit, he launches from the bed to the dresser, crashing into the front of it like he was thrown into it.

The dresser rocks from the impact and the drawers slide out as Mason lies on the carpet. As horrified as he is, Dante still races to his son's side to be an attentive father. Mason sees him. "No! Stop!" he screams, scooting away from his father and backing into the corner of his room. His hands in front of him in defense.

"I just want to help, let me see you son," Dante says, approaching him.

Mason passes out and is unresponsive. The silence in the room is so quiet that there is an indescribable ringing in Dante's ears. He kneels beside Mason and notices him still breathing. Dante is relieved at the sight of breathing but the fear and adrenaline is still feeding his body to act. Mason lies on the floor, seemingly fine, only a low guttural sound hums from the boy. Dante goes back to his side to listen closer and see if maybe he is awake but before he could get too close, the lights in the room flicker on. The overhead light bulb glows and as Dante turns to look into it, it glows brighter and brighter just before popping. Shards of glass rain down onto the bed and small pieces explode onto the carpet as Dante shields himself from the sudden sound.

Being a man of faith, and pastor, Dante has heard of stories that are all too familiar to what just happened.

Something evil is present.

The realization makes his heart sink into the pit of his stomach and he backs out of the room. He pulls the door closed and his back hits the wall as he slides down it and buries his face into his hands and cries.

Chapter Fourteen

Dante wears out the kitchen floor, pacing anxiously. The thoughts collide in his mind like wet clay that only splashes and drips as it fails to hold its shape. *What was that up there?* he thinks. Seeing his boy's bones buckle and break in their twisting deformation was as unsettling as some of the stories in that holy book he reads passages from each week. Why does a well-cared for, and abundantly-loved child spew such hatred?

Why does he suddenly show such blatant disregard for his father?

Why do his words dig their way into his brain and somehow send cracks through Dante's heart?

Why do his eyes feel like rage from someone else?

Feeling that sting from Mason's verbal assault will undoubtedly leave scars on Dante's psyche, but as a loving father, seeing what was happening to his son put his heart in a chokehold. Wanting to help and be attentive is one thing, but feeling helpless coupled with the inability to respond properly is another.

Dante's world is rocked, like a small rowboat in a sea of dark water under the cloud-hidden moonlight.

No help in any direction.

An absence of light to guide him home.

No one to answer no matter how many times or how loud he screams into the vast and empty distance.

Dante likens himself as more of a sinking rock in that sea though, after witnessing his child in distress and being unable to cure what ails him. Truly a nightmare scenario for any parent.

What now?

All of these questions plague Dante as he patrols the lower level of his house after eleven in the evening. Dante knows what is happening in his heart and in his mind. Those stories in that book, the things he has heard over the years, the taboo nature of demons existing and latching onto humans like some sort of fleas from hell that turn loved ones into evil people.

The idea of meditating again crosses his mind and is quickly disregarded. This seems more urgent, and deep belly breathing hardly seems like a practical solution. Dante considered calling nine-one-one after Mason launched himself into the dresser. He didn't respond in pain afterward, but he did fall asleep on the floor.

Could be a concussion. Grace suggested it before and he practically laughed it off but after seeing first-hand, maybe it is worth exploring. Maybe it is better to be naive and pray that this isn't what he thinks it is. What doesn't make sense though is that Mason was showing signs of irritation before that, so Dante, once again brushes aside the possibility of a concussion.

Possession.

In the back of his mind, he also worries how this may look if he calls paramedics. People will think he can't take care of his son. And what if Mason tells doctors unfavorable things? After the day they've had, unpredictability seems too risky for the investigation and questioning of child welfare that would surely follow. *I should go check on him first and see if he has injuries,* he thinks. *Maybe it's not that bad. Maybe I'm just tired.*

Still a bit shaken and hesitant to go back into Mason's room, he considers calling Grace but realizes the time. *She is probably in bed or busy. I've bothered her enough,* he thinks. With his phone in hand, he stares at her name on the screen, thumb hovering, ready to call. His nervous feet trudge along the floor, with the weight of each step booming through the quiet house. Too many thoughts to feel confident about any responsible decision-making. He anticipates how the phone call might go if he does call her. Anxiety has reared its ugly head and the question to solution ratio is not great.

He expects that he will tell her what happened and she won't believe everything. What sane and sensible person would? Especially with their child involved. The two will bicker for a moment before Dante gets quiet and Grace will suggest that their boy is just growing up. Dante will disagree, Grace will offer to come get him, and Dante will be too proud of a dad to allow her to make him feel incapable of being a parent, and nothing will be accomplished when they end the call.

He sets the phone on the countertop and goes to his computer in the dining room. Logging in, he goes directly to Facebook and sees a bunch of notifications on his last live post. Without even checking them he prepares to 'go live' once more. Despite his appearance being less than presentable, he clicks the red dot and now he is live-streaming to his audience, made up mostly of church members and some family and friends.

Dante sits for a moment, not really saying much of anything. He runs his hand through his hair a few times and rubs his eyes every bit as uncomfortable as the feed might suggest to anyone watching.

Why am I even doing this now?

He buttons the top buttons of his soiled and wrinkled shirt, recognizing that he should have changed, but this spontaneous deed is a *right now* sort of thing.

He smacks his hands together and centers himself with the web-cam. Rubbing his palms together he relaxes his face, but ironically it feels like a mask to him. "Good evening everyone," he begins. The number of active watchers climbs in a hurry. Messages pop up along with *thumbs up* and *heart* emojis. "I hope everyone is having themselves a great weekend. I know that," Dante stares off camera and pauses.

Why are you up so late, pastor?

Looking forward to the luncheon tomorrow.

We should hang out sometime.

Several messages pop up, but Dante ignores them. In fact, he doesn't even read them out loud to even give an opportunity to respond. He came to this stream with a purpose and he is beginning to wonder if he should just sign off. "I know that it's late, and I know this is a strange time for me to do this." He chortles, shaking his head as the uncertainty of his words rattle around in his head. "You all are used to me doing this when the sun is up. I know we all got service in the morning and a big day with the luncheon but I thought this might be a good opportunity to share with you all. You all are my community. Neighbors. Friends. Family. Today, for me ... personally, was not a great day. My son, Mason ... him and I have met with ... conflict."

More messages dance onto the screen.

What's going on with Mason?

R U guys OK?

I think I saw you two at the park earlier.

Let me know if you guys need anything.

"I'm reaching out to you, my people, simply asking that you say a prayer for my boy. Say a prayer the same way everyone would for you if you were facing hardship, lost loved ones, sickness, or anything else that weighs heavy on your heart through the day. If you could do that for me, I would be blessed and grateful for your thoughts."

I'll pray for you, pastor.

Are you going to be at church tomorrow?

I hope Mason is okay. Such a sweet boy.

"Getting back to Mason, now, his mother says it's just that he is at *that* age, but I believe there is more to it. Now I don't wanna go into it much more than that, but I thought this was a great time to be vulnerable. So many of you look to me for guidance and wisdom, and despite my role," Dante drops his head low for a moment. When he raises it, his eyes are glassy and the well is not dry. He clears his ragged throat. "Despite my role, I'm just a guy. I'm just a normal human. A normal child of God just like all of you. I face challenges in my own private life and I deal with real problems that create strife. At the end of the day though, when I'm getting ready to lay my head down in my warm bed, I reflect and I talk to God. I maintain my personal relationship with Him and I put my faith in Him. He will place me where I am meant to be. The same way He will for you ... all you gotta do is just talk to Him."

God is good, all the time!

It's ok to not be ok pastor.

Will there be vegetarian stuff to eat tomorrow?

You're a great pastor and I love coming to your sermons.

Dante dries his eyes with the back of his hand and clears his nasal passages. "That's all I got," he says with a laugh and forced smile. His baggy eyes as red as his flushed cheeks stare into the camera. "Got a big day tomorrow. Get some rest. I'll see you all in church tomorrow. Good night."

Dante signs off, the stream ends and he makes his way upstairs. The bed calls his name but it is important that he checks on Mason.

Tap, tap, tap on the door before he eases into the room. The glass remains on the carpet under the mandatory darkness. In an odd turn of events, Mason is in his bed, underneath the covers sleeping soundly. His breathing seems normal enough to eradicate any further concerns.

Dante creeps in, stepping around the glimmering shards of glass he can see, and dusts off the comforter of glass before sitting beside Mason's sleeping back. The shaken father watches his bothered boy sleep in peace as his hand rubs his back, just like he did regularly when he was smaller. Like he did when he didn't try to hurt him. Dante inspects his shoulders and feels around his arms looking for signs of broken bones, or even a slight reaction to his touch. Mason sleeps soundly, unharmed as if it hadn't even happened. *I don't understand,* he thinks, eyes fixated on the light from the window reflecting on the broken glass that glitters in the carpet. Fingers run through the boy's messy hair and he is unflinching and dreaming, or so Dante hopes.

He stands after a few moments and stares at his son. "Good night, son. I love you. Sleep tight," he whispers, following a soft kiss on the forehead. Dancing around the shards of glass, he leaves the room. The door pulls closed and Dante meanders to his room where he says a silent prayer to the God he has questioned more than he is proud of lately. The silent prayer transitions into his knees on the floor and his elbows on the side of his bed as he stares at the ceiling.

"God, I know this is just you testing me, and I know you're all-knowing and that I've been a fraud. I don't deserve to be an extension of your message, but I know if you're there that you understand me." Dante's tears flow freely down his cheek as he has given up the fight thanks to the privacy of his bedroom and lack of an audience. "You know that my intentions are good, Lord. I need you to put me where I belong. I know in my heart this isn't it. I can't do this anymore."

Dante idles at his bedside, his chest rattling with each breath. "I need my son to be okay. I don't know what's wrong with him but I know you have a plan for him. But that's my son in there and I just ... I just need to know he's gonna be fine. I don't know what I would do if something happened."

Dante looks at the clock on his night stand and sees the time. It's just after midnight. His bed extends the invitation to rest and he crawls into it, hopeful that the day to follow is better.

CHAPTER FIFTEEN

SUNDAY

Dante's legs push through the bottom of the blanket as his restless body stirs. Resisting the waking of his body, his attempts to roll over are constricted by a feeling of tightness. A feeling of weight on his chest. Only being half awake, he fights to move only to fail. His lungs only take in a portion of his deep breath and the labored breathing is enough to sound alarms. His eyes open to Mason, sitting on his chest with his legs crossed, and his full weight perched on Dante, studying him.

Surprise widens Dante's eyes upon waking and he stills his movement. "Mason," he whispers under the canopy of darkness. Mason's head pivots to the side slowly, like a dog behind a fence being taunted by a peculiar noise.

"What are you doing, son?" Dante asks, the words shaking as bad as he is. Mason's head raises upright and tilts back as his arms spread wide like Jesus on the cross. His head rocks forward with the blackened eyes and glassy stare that shakes Dante to his core. Fear is in the driver's seat now and Mason's outstretched arms bend and pop, and the joints in his wrist follow suit with the sounds of cartilage crunching to the dislocating of bone. Mason's head jerks back hard as if someone pulled his hair and he begins to groan. The sound starts as a low murmur and becomes a deep call from the pit of his stomach. The bass from the throaty hum grows and becomes louder. The more Dante lays transfixed on what's happening, the more deafening the vibrations from Mason evolve.

The sound becomes unbearable as Dante scoots and forces himself from underneath his son, his sleepy body smashes against the floor while Mason remains in the same seated position, unbothered. The noise continues to grow as Dante stumbles to his feet with his hands pressed over his ears. "Mason!" he screams, attempting to yell over the sound coming from his son. "Mason!" he shouts even louder as he falls into the wall and flips the light switch. The room illuminates a soft light and the noise ceases instantly as Mason's suddenly relaxed body collapses, nearly falling off the bed.

Dante rushes to his side, rolling him onto his back to see his face. He taps his cheeks softly. "Mason, wake up," he smacks him gently three more times. "Mason!" He shakes the boy and cradles his head in his arms. "Wake up, wake up! Please wake up!"

Mason's eyes flicker to life and a spark renders his face surprised.

"I gotcha, it's okay, I gotcha."

Mason's eyes crawl around his dad's room, disoriented and lost.

"Everything is fine. It was just–"

Mason jerks away, scurrying to the floor. He scoots away from his father until he is in a corner, scared, with his knees pulled to his chin, tight. He shivers like an abused dog without breaking his gaze from his father.

"What's wrong?" Dante asks. "Why are you lookin' at me like that?"

Mason tenses up, yet still refuses to take his eyes away from his father.

"Are you hurt? I can call the ambulance if you're hurt," Dante offers.

Mason sits, curled into a tightly wound ball shaking his head *no*.

"Okay," Dante says. "How about some water? Are you thirsty?"

Mason stares, not acknowledging, but not denying.

"Stay put, I'll go get you some water."

Dante walks downstairs and fills a clear glass at the kitchen sink and brings it back up. He extends the glass of water to Mason who doesn't reach for it.

"Here ... take it."

No response, no reaction as Mason watches his father with the offering held within reach.

Dante stands with his arm out and looks at the time on the alarm clock on his night stand. The glowing red numbers showing 1:08 A.M.

He sets the glass at Mason's feet and he sits on the floor beside him. "I'm not going to hurt you or do anything son ... I don't know why you're so shaky right now. I love you Mason." Mason tenses up but breaks his stare and looks at the water. "You've just gotta relax." Dante throws an arm around Mason's shoulders and pulls him closer and hugs him in an awkward side by side position. They sit like this until eventually the two doze off. Dante catches himself dozing and raises his head. He adjusts himself and lays Mason down gently onto the floor. He grabs the pillow from his bed and grabs a fleece blanket to cover him up and lets him sleep where he is.

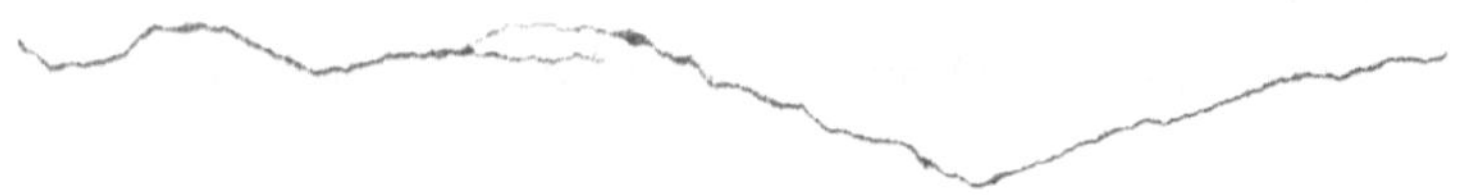

Standing at his bathroom sink, the exhaustion clings to his skin. It seeps into his flesh as he rinses it off of his face with frigid water. His reflection stares back at him, a red-eyed doppelganger of himself on his worst day. It's 3 A.M. and he knows that tomorrow is going to be a long day of dragging himself around with fake smiles and absent-minded interactions. In addition to the sermon that he would be doing, he also has the luncheon afterward that will require more of his time and energy.

Talk about timing, if I ever needed to sleep more than I do right now, he thinks as he gives up on the idea of sleeping and leans into the rush of adrenaline that overrides the idea of trying to doze off. The burst of energy sends Dante back downstairs where he does meaningless tasks around the house that could most definitely wait until tomorrow. The idea of sleeping is appealing but the risk of oversleeping is not worth taking so he fiddles with mostly unproductive things downstairs. Things that make him feel at ease in the moment.

The low light from the overhead puck lights reflect off of the smooth and very clean surface of the kitchen counter. Dante paces with a rag and bottle of cleaning product. He has wiped down the microwave and the stove. He considers cleaning the floor but remembers there is laundry downstairs that he can start and feasibly get into the dryer before they have to get ready for church. He marches from room to room tossing loose clothing into a laundry basket and finds his way into the basement.

He flips the switch at the top of the steps and the bulbs stutter and brighten as he makes the descent into the laundry room, more akin to a dungeon. The fluorescent bulbs buzz and flicker like darkness scratching at the room as he loads the washing machine. Once he has started the washer, the light strobes. He turns to see it just as it goes dark. The door upstairs from the kitchen feeds light in from the stairway but is blocked by a silhouette. Mason is standing there, atop the steps with the light at his back, leering into the basement.

Chapter Sixteen

Dante takes careful steps toward the shadowy figure atop the stairs that stands in the threshold. Mason stands as still as stone with eyes fixed on his father. Dante's eyes squint to focus with a hand over his eyes like a visor. "I'm surprised you're awake, son."

Mason's head drops to the side. "You've let everyone down, Dante," an unsettling, yet cheerful voice rings out. "It's time to put *your* feet to the fire now."

Dante stops where he stands, his hand drops from his face, now wearing confusion and horror in his expression. "What's that, buddy?"

A sickening smirk creeps onto the boy's face. "I'm sorry ... your little buddy isn't here anymore."

Dante paces to the base of the steps. "Okay ... if he isn't here, then where is he?"

"He is sleeping now," the voice says, deeper than before, sounding nothing like Mason at all. A voice that carries from the belly and roars throughout his body. Faster than Dante can blink, Mason lunges from the top of the stairs and crashes into him as they both hit the floor. Mason shrieks and wails as he scurries to mount his father who lies on his back. Dante tries to defend and ward off the flurry of hands that claw and beg to grip his throat. His fighting becomes exhausting as Mason's aggression is not that of a boy, but the strength of a man. Something more visceral and unfamiliar.

Mason overtakes his father and throttles his neck, fingernails digging to the point of drawing blood. The boy's arms and muscles tense up, and his head is still with his jaw clenched and teeth bare. His breathing sounds like a hungry stomach as he purrs, eyes turning that deep black, just like before. Dante continues to fight and overpower his son but he is just too strong. Desperate for air and to be free of the fingernails tearing more into his flesh, he is in fear for his life.

In the interest of living, Dante's legs kick as his hips buck while he tries to slip from beneath the boy. Mason's mechanical grip is firm until Dante is able to grab his wrist and dislocate the elbow. *POP!*

The grip is released and Dante scurries away on his ass, pushing away with his feet until his back is against the washing machine that hums and swooshes as a soundtrack to the chaos happening in the basement.

Mason staggers away, hissing and growling before collapsing to the floor. "Please don't hurt me!" he begs, the voice of Mason, the innocent son of Dante. "Why are you trying to hurt me, Dad?" he asks through muffled cries. The boy steps into the light with tear streaks on his cheeks as he violently pops the elbow back into place with a grunt. "I thought you loved me, Daddy!" he shouts. "Why don't you love me anymore, Daddy!?" as his voice returns to the deep tone of whatever beast Mason has become.

With an outstretched arm that points at Dante, and a face that portrays only malice, an assortment of items lying around the basement are sent flying toward Dante. Much like a gust of wind hurling yard items into fixed structures; tools, a laundry basket of clothes, various other items from shelves are sent into the wall at high velocity. Metal bangs against the washer and dryer, tools clang against the cinderblock wall behind the appliances, and Dante flinches, trying to protect himself from the supernatural assault.

Mason slides across the floor, tackling his father. Dante and Mason wrestle for control. The boy with soulless eyes scuffling to maim his father spews hateful words. "You've always been a shit father. Look at you! It's no wonder you're trying to hurt me now!"

Dante ignores the words with only one goal in mind: escape.

Fearful in a way that makes him tremble, unlike any other time in his life, he recognizes that something unholy is happening in his home and getting away to seek help is the only thing to be done. The pastor has only heard stories of this sort of thing but the idea of possession has crossed his mind over the course of the last few hours. The thought seemed silly at first and was disregarded immediately. The level of aggression that pummels him now has only further cemented the notion that his sweet boy has been taken by a demonic entity and it aims to hurt him.

"You fight like a coward, holy man!" the boy taunts, continuing to push and tangle with the pastor.

Dante puts his all into pushing his son back until Mason is pressed against the HVAC system. "You can't have my son!" Dante says thoughtlessly, as he bangs the beast against the unit. The handcuffs that they use for playing cops and robbers rattle and scrape against one of the attached pipes and in a knee-jerk reaction, Dante grabs the open cuff and slaps it onto Mason's wrist and falls back, away from the now captured boy.

Mason pulls and panics, matching Dante's own heightened response. Trying to break free from the long chain that is secured to the air conditioning system, Mason realizes he is restrained and vulnerable. The effort to be free continues; growling and yelling, cursing and flailing, he yanks on the cuffs destructively, actively destroying nothing, only making a lot of noise.

Dante sits against the wall, across from Mason, just watching the distress of his son, or what *used* to be his son. With his heart rate climbing and the tension maxed out, he watches the boy try to pull and slide his hand from the tight cuff on his wrist. The desire to roam free is like watching a dog caught in a bear trap as it chews off its leg to escape. Blood is drawn and trickles down his arm as he pulls relentlessly and the chain on the cuffs is taut. His face grimaces and then the effort to slip out of the cuffs ceases.

"Release me at once, holy man!" the beast commands.

Dante sits, shaking his head *no*, unwilling to be bullied by a demon. "No!" he answers.

The boy's mouth unhinges and a screech rings out that defies Dante's refusal to obey the demon's demand. Dante rushes to his feet and with his ears covered flees the basement, storming up the stairs before the beast quiets the screeching. Standing at the top of the stairs, he turns back to see Mason creeping into the light that shines down from the kitchen. He stares up at his father, with one arm pulled back, thanks to the arrest.

Part II

Arrested For Possession

Chapter Seventeen

"No, no, no, no, crap!" Dante mutters into the lonely kitchen. The sunless morning creeps into the house as he tries not to hyperventilate. "What even was that? What just happened?"

The calm on the main floor may feel safe, but the sounds of his pacing and panicked breathing don't drown out the boy ... the ... thing ... crying downstairs. "Dad!" the voice cries from below. Cries that reach up the stairs and foster themselves into Dante's heart. "Please let me out. I promise I'll be good, Dad!" Mason's voice whines. "I'll be good!"

Dante leans over the kitchen sink and turns on the faucet and drinks directly from the water filling his hands. Several gulps of water and splashes to his face that follow remind him just how awake he is and the reality of his situation that's taking root. "Dammit!" he says, smacking his palm against the counter hard enough to make the dishes in the cabinet rattle. Energy with no purpose has him wound up. He hangs his head in his hand and tries to meditate in the moment. The breathing exercise fails as quickly as it begins. The weight of the recent events have created questions that break the focus of meditation.

Okay, my son is in the basement, chained to the furnace. "What to do, what to do?" he asks aloud. He smacks himself in the forehead three times in succession. "Think, think, think!"

He runs through the scenario and the hypothetical outcomes in his mind. The goal is to figure out what is going on with Mason first, then to get him safely out of the basement and ensure he is calm. The delicate topic of why he handcuffed his son to the furnace in the wee hours of the morning is a tricky piece to explain to his mother though. One he prefers not to ever mention, considering that news travels fast in this town and he cannot fathom the town judging him as a father. *They don't know what is happening here, they would have done the same,* he thinks.

How can he slip out of this situation without looking like an abusive father, a horrible parent, and a hypocrite?

How can he maintain his clean image as being a servant of God?

This isn't the sort of thing that people just forgive and let go. This will be something gossiped about. The idea of whispers in the pews every Sunday only fill him with dread. Friendly greetings in supermarkets become forced smiles and shifty eyes.

How does this affect Mason? Dante thinks.

Could he actually be possessed? The thought seems silly to Dante, albeit warranted to at least consider. Even worse, *what if he isn't possessed?* Dante ponders.

What if there is something medically wrong with him and I'm just wasting time chasing demons.

Maybe this divorce has been harder on Mason than he has let on in the last year.

The questions and inner monologue only make things worse. Dante has a strong feeling that some demonic force has nestled its way into his son and something will need to be done. Something drastic.

Dante drops to his knees with his hands clasped together in prayer. His eyes are fixed to the ceiling as they begin to water. He begins to pray. "God ... please ... something has a hold of my boy ...

please don't let this happen. I need you, God!" he begs, fighting back tears that still manage to shake his voice. "Amen."

As he stands up he can hear Mason, still calling out, "Dad!? Please!"

He looks at the clock and sees that it is almost 3:30 A.M. He has a sermon to deliver in less than five hours and a big luncheon to follow. He was supposed to take care of things that he is just not thinking about. Things that were not tended to. The sermon wasn't exactly the kind of job you could just call off from, at least that was Dante's mentality when it came to the church.

His busy body marches to the computer in the dining room. He logs on to the church's Facebook account. Earlier in the day he posted a graphic for the event, welcoming everyone and their families to come for food, drinks, and a good time. He clicks the notifications and right on top, he sees Susan's name and face. He views the comments on the post.

Mister Dante, I went ahead and picked up some plasticware anyway. I can't wait to see everybody Sunday! God bless.

As annoyed at her comment and incessant need to insert herself as useful when she was told directly not to, he is glad she picked up the plasticware since he failed to. Others comment and have shared the post but he pays little mind to them. He looks at the last video he posted and sees even more comments telling him to hang in there and that he is in their thoughts and prayers. Dante begins to compose a post but after he types a single sentence he thinks better of it and deletes the draft.

He sits at his desk, wrapped in thoughts that lead to questions. Questions that lead to no answers. Well, at least no answers that don't absolutely terrify him. "What am I going to tell Grace?" he asks. *And Mason, what is he going to think about me after tonight? Who does this to their child?*

The only thing that he is certain of is that Grace cannot know about this. The thought of her berating him and cutting him down even more as a failed partner and even worse father makes him unsteady on his feet, so he sits. Light-headedness skips merrily through his darkest fear, one he didn't even know he had, alongside the feeling of his stomach clawing up his throat. The feeling that keeps him from speaking, but also from screaming.

After several minutes, the feeling passes and he stands. Addressing this head-on may be the only option. Mason has calmed after calling up for his father for so long only to be ignored. Dante inches to the open basement door where he stands atop the steps peering into the basement. Chills scour his body like waves of ice just under his skin as his eyes adjust to the darkness downstairs. The light pours in, only lighting the landing of the steps. Silence stares back at him as the shivers crawl. The absence of God makes the home feel even more desolate. Dante hangs onto the hope that God works in mysterious ways, but all things considered in the moment, he is struggling to believe. Where faith wavers, words do too, his gasps just as ragged as his nerves.

"Mason," he says, quavering.

There is pause in the silence while he awaits a response. Any kind of response. His anxiety is at its peak, that is before the sound of the handcuffs drag and scrape along the pipe. Mason creeps into the light, his arm stretched back dramatically as his steps are brought to a stop. His head leans forward as he tilts his head to look upstairs.

Mason says nothing.

Dante begins the slow descent, inching down the staircase, closer to the empty stare of his son's standing there.

His feet hit the concrete landing and Mason shuffles away and cowers against the wall, whimpering with his face buried between his knees. His arm raised in a position that *must* be uncomfortable.

Dante keeps his back to the wall directly across from the HVAC system that Mason is imprisoned to. He is careful to maintain a safe distance from any outbursts Mason might have. Slow, sideways strides and an attempt to not look defensive only make Dante look more afraid and guarded as he traverses further from the steps, and further from the light.

"Son," he whispers. "Mason … please, just talk to me."

Mason adjusts his body and lifts his head, staring at his father, with just a single eye visible above his knees.

Dante drags a hand through his hair and pushes out a held breath from his nostrils. "I'm so sorry, son … I didn't mean to- I-," he stumbles through his apology. Thoughts broken into pieces, similar to what his life has been lately. "I hope you can forgive me, son … I'm gonna get you out of here. You're gonna be okay."

He leans against the wall and slides down, his bottom hitting the cold cement floor. He looks around the basement, this is no condition for a child. The smell becomes more noticeable as he is closer to the floor. The smell of cold moisture living in the bricks, saturating the floor. Water sitting in the drain with the mildew scent that only an unfinished basement can offer. "You know, this last year has been really tough on me, kiddo … I know it's been hard on you too, even if you don't see it yet. But I'm tryin'. Your mother is tryin'."

Dante looks over to Mason and sees his head raised. Face shown, meeting his eyes like he is listening.

"I never wanted this for you. If it were up to me, your mother and I would still be together and you wouldn't have to go between houses … I've not handled my family being torn apart as well as I make it seem … and I've been so stressed out with the church and trying to just keep things moving along. I thought I found my purpose … but somewhere along the way I lost my family."

The chain shakes and clinks against the pipe as Mason rises to his feet. Dante stands as well.

"You know ... I just haven't been okay ever since–"

"Ever since grandpa died?" Mason cuts in. Dante's face fills with color and his eyes light up at the sound of his son's innocent voice.

"Yes. Ever since grandpa passed and I had to fill his shoes, I've just been treading water to barely stay afloat. If I'm being honest, I'm not sure I was ready to take over. And to be even more honest, I don't know that I wanted this for myself."

"Do you think that's why grandpa died?"

"What do you mean?"

"To get away from you?"

The color in Dante's face becomes red nearly as fast as he could accept what is happening. "Why would you say that to me?"

A wide grin pulls across Mason's face and he bends his knees like a bouncing toy as he slides the cuff across the pipe. The scraping noise is a disorienting percussion joined by his laughter. Dante backs away, frightened just enough to match his dismay.

Mason's soft boyish voice deepens into a growling cackle. Something much more insidious. "He had to get away from his failure of a son!" he says in a sing-song kind of way with the metal scraping metal and his neck bending each way to every word. The laughter and the singing stops. His knees straighten and he tenses up, yanking hard on the cuffs with his fiery stare burning through Dante who cowers in the dark. "It's funny, he is dead, but you still live in his shadow."

Dante feels a panic attack creeping in and rushes for the stairs past the beast that he doesn't believe is his son. Mason swipes at his father with bare teeth clenched and a monster's purr that vibrates off of the walls of the basement. Heavy feet storm up the steps and Dante slips on the polished floor planks as he gets up the steps. From his knees, his legs fight to perform simple things, like standing, or crawling, making him a skittering mess of limbs. He reels from the floor and pulls himself onto a chair at the table. Weary from running, he watches the open door to the basement. Sweaty and fatigued he offers another prayer. "Please God, Jesus, I need you, I need you. I need strength. Please grant me the courage to face this demon. I need to get my boy back. Please save him from this fiend that has my boy," he whispers.

"Oh Dante," a voice calls from below. Dante recognizes the voice immediately, but is in disbelief. "Hey! ... Donno! Why don't you come down here, say hello to ya old man, would'ja?"

The room practically closes in at the voice of Dante's father. *Nobody calls me Donno.*

"What are you doin' up there anyway, boy?"

"You're not real!" Dante shouts. He walks over and slams the door shut.

The voice booms through the house, paying no mind to the closed door, or physics for that matter. "You've gotta be kiddin' me. Donno, come down here, right now! You're gonna be in big trouble when I get home, boy!" The voice is exactly as he remembers. The gravelly and raspy voice that preached goodness and praised the Lord. "Figures you're too chicken. I ain't seen't'cha since my funeral, you'd think you'd be happy to come see me. But noooo, Donno is too busy, failing as a husband." Dante's fingers curl and form a tight fist. "Look atcha, you let Grace down ... you took my church from me and what? You run it into the ground!? I thought I taught you better, boy!" The seething voice and poisonous words cut through Dante enough to override the fear. Blinded by a growing anger he stands near the door. "You're gonna let all of these people down too. Just like you're lettin' ya son down. Just like you're lettin' down that God you just prayed to ... you know, you really did grow up to be a pathetic piece of work."

"Shut up!" Dante demands, speaking over the voice of his father, ranting.

"You've got my grandson chained up to a damn furnace! Who chains up their own child to a furnace?"

Dante pounds on the door, battering repeatedly, "Shut up! Shut up! Shut up!"

"Hey! Stop all that yellin'! You're scarin' little Mason."

Dante turns away and heads for the back door. Fresh air is needed more than ever. "Yeah, no one is surprised. Turn and run away from ya problems. Just like ya always do!"

The door swings open and Dante falls forward onto his patio, collapsing into the cold and calm cement. A moment of reprieve is the closest thing he has had to a blessing all night. But now it is almost morning and the sky is pink and orange with deep shades of purple as the morning sun ganders at an early Sunday. It isn't quite meditating, but the birds chirping and singing–that he usually finds annoying–are a welcome sound. Every breath of cool air fills his lungs and he has a moment to clear his mind. No voices from the basement seem to bother him outside. Further proof that something is very wrong inside that house.

Chapter Eighteen

S itting in a flowerbed, ass firmly seeped in mulch, Dante revels in the calm breeze and nature happening around him. It isn't long before the peace is broken by the sound of a storm door slamming shut.

"Leave it, I'll get it, hun," Barry says to his wife.

Dante stands, patting himself off, ridding his messy shirt and pants of debris and mulch. It hardly helps to make him look any less unkempt. He looks around for a place to hide, hoping not to be seen by his chatty neighbor. Curiosity keeps him from doing so as he raises his head to look over a hedge on the side yard where he sees Barry carrying a cooler and various items for a cookout into his Equinox. He keeps the tailgate up as he loads it.

As Barry turns to go back into the house he catches a glimpse of Dante staring at him.

"Hey there, neighbor," Barry greets, with a tempered chuckle. "You alright over there?"

"Everything's fine," Dante replies, too quickly to seem like things are fine.

Barry strolls back, alongside the fence that is parallel to the side of the house. "You sure, neighbor?" he asks, not trying to hide his suspicion as he looks him up and down. "Because you look like shit, Dante."

"It's just been–" Dante starts, gesturing his filthy hands to the house.

"Are you not going to church this morning? A little early for you to be out here gardening, isn't it?"

Dante turns to see the flower bed he was sitting in and sees a pile of weeds he must have been picking without realizing. He rubs the back of his neck. "Yeah, just having trouble sleeping for some reason. I hope I didn't wake–"

"No, no, not at all!" Barry assures. "I was already up. Barb likes to get up early anyhow and have her coffee and quiet. I was just gettin' ready to roll out here in a few."

"Where're you heading off to this early?"

"Georgetown. Meeting some of the guys down there this morning to tailgate. I figured I'd get a head start."

"What's in Georgetown?"

"Who Dey, baby! Bengals practice before the season. Gonna watch Joe Burrow throw some bombs, if he can stay on the field." Barry laughs at himself.

Not one to follow local sports too closely, the humor goes over Dante's head. "Well, go team."

"You don't follow too much football, I take it?"

The conversation is just neighborly drabble that is only raising the possibility that Dante will tip off any suspicions. He begins to try and ease out of the conversation but Barry continues to rattle off stats about the Bengals and what the analysts are saying on SportsCenter. Dante couldn't care less on a normal day, but today is not a normal day.

"They should be able to take the division this year. Just got to stay healthy and keep guys on the field. You should tag along to a game this year, bring Mason and we can–"

Barry's words become background noise to the immediate problem that is on the forefront of Dante's mind.

The child who was *arrested for possession* in the basement.

Dante's mind is moving a million miles a minute as the anxiety projects improbable scenarios with the occasional one that could happen. Like *what if Mason were to scream right now? Would Barry hear it?*

"Oh no!" Dante says, interrupting Barry.

Puzzled, Barry is taken aback. "Alright, alright, that's enough about football."

"What?" Dante stammers, not meaning to have spoken his thoughts aloud. "No, it's not that, I just … It's been a long night and I'm just–"

"Tired, I get'cha."

"Yeah. I just have a lot on my mind."

"Woman problems?" Barry asks with all of the machismo of a manly man.

Dante chooses not to answer, seeing the intrusive question as a segway. "Have a good night, or morning. Enjoy the game," he says, turning to go back into the house. "Say hello to Barb for me."

"Take care, neighbor," Barry says, watching Dante sulk back to the house. "Don't pray too hard," he says with a hearty chuckle.

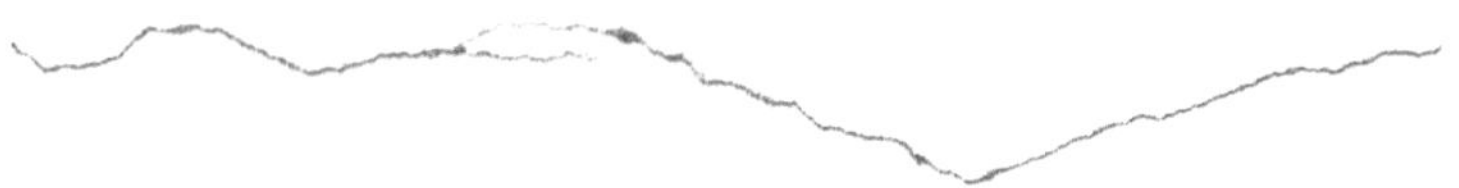

Dante is passed out at the dinner table, slumped over with his head laid down like a high school student sleeping through the first bell. He stirs just enough for his arm to slip off of the side and jar him awake. With his hair a mess, and drool on his forearm and face, he is dumbstruck for a moment as he sees the time and stands in a hurry.

The only way Dante knows how to operate is to maintain his routines. Every Sunday before church he makes breakfast and will do ordinary things and typically be well put together. This morning, however, is not a routine morning. Beginning with him waking up later than he normally would to get started with the day, he had no intentions of falling asleep. The other thing is that he has not changed or showered so he is already behind on cleanliness. Is cleanliness still Godliness when there is possibly a demon in the basement? All of this compounding with the fact that church starts in nearly an hour and on a normal Sunday they would be leaving shortly with plans to arrive early.

Instead, Dante is rushing around the kitchen with breakfast still in mind, hoping to feed Mason and himself despite every-thing. Dante opens the basement door to a response of the chain rattling gently. "Mason ... son?"

Dante heads down, stopping halfway to see Mason leaning against the wall, legs stretched out, and his head leaning into his shoulder where his hand is suspended above his head. "Mason?" Dante beckons in a hushed voice.

The silence hangs for just a moment before it is broken by light snoring. *I'll let him sleep a while longer,* Dante thinks as he heads back up to the kitchen.

He scrambles some eggs in a skillet. While those are going he microwaves some cheap sausage links that come in a box. Stirring the eggs every few seconds he manages to pop a couple pieces of bread into the toaster. So far, so good, in terms of the routine. He prepares two plates and gets two sets of silverware and pauses. He looks at the second set and thinks better of it, and puts it back.

Dante opens the basement door, letting it creak open slowly as the kitchen light spills down the stairs. He makes his way down, slowly with a plate in each hand. "Mason," he whispers. As he gets to the bottom he says it again. "Mason ... time to get up, bud."

The chains jingle and bang on the pipe. Mason stirs in his sleep. Passed out on the floor, cold against bare skin, with his arm elevated in an awkward position. His wrists are bruised and bent and the white tank top he went to bed in is absolutely filthy now. His head is lulled to the side. Dried tear streaks break the grease and grime on his face as he sits there.

Dante places the plate of food on the floor and scoots it toward Mason with his foot. He backs away and hollers, "Mason, wake up ... I made you breakfast."

Mason's eyelids flutter and open and he looks at his dad, repulsed and surprised.

"You should eat."

Mason just stares at the food. His eyes dance between his own plate and the one his father is leaning over on the dryer as he cuts a piece of sausage with the side of the fork. "You want me to get you some orange juice or something?" he asks, still chewing. "I can bring you down some water, I think there is some apple juice even."

Mason studies the plate on the floor with a cold stare. "Why can't I just go upstairs and get it myself?" he asks, watching his father eat. "I'm sorry for last night. I don't know what I did," he says, tears dampening his words more. "I promise, Dad, I'll be good. We can go to church."

Dante stares at the ceiling with watering eyes, choking back any response.

"I miss mommy." The boy begins to let go, pulling his knees and free arm to his face as he whimpers.

Dante walks over and kneels beside him, setting the plate and fork on the floor. His arms wrap around his son and swallow him up in an embrace that allows him to forget about everything that has happened in the last twelve hours.

"I'm so sorry son," Dante cries in what is the most normal and genuine moment he has felt this morning.

CHAPTER NINETEEN

"You can take off the cuffs now, dad," Mason says, raising his head enough to show his face.

Dante pulls away, still suspicious of the boy. "Do you remember what happened last night?"

"Why can't I have a fork? You want me to eat with my hand?" Dante rests a comforting hand on his son's shoulder. "You're keeping me down here like some sort of bad dog. Just let me out...please, Dad."

With a long sigh, Dante looks away. "I can't do that, son. I'm sorry."

Mason's head sinks back into his knees as the silence hangs between them. "You're going to be sorry," Mason whispers.

"What's that?" Dante asks, knowing exactly what he heard, but desperate to not believe it.

Mason's calm body jerks and in an agitated burst of excitement he pulls on his secured arm as if to slip through the cuffs. The metal noise rings out as Mason stands. "Let me out! Let me out! Let me *out*!"

His teeth grit as his muscles tighten and twist. Dante shuffles away toward the steps as Mason's spectacle returns. Tendons strain and veins bulge from the boy's neck. His head rotates slowly, like he is exercising the full range of motion while a nasally hum emanates from the throat. His head rocks forward, frightening Dante enough to flinch as black eyes lock onto him. The pastor can see his reflection in the light from upstairs pouring into the darkness of Mason's eyes. He can see just how out of sorts Mason is. The eyes are deep. There is a loneliness to them that feels cold. But something about that deepness feels like hell. Maybe hell isn't all fire and brimstone like the *good ole book* says. Maybe it's lonely, dark, and damp while being just as frigid as the chill that is intermingling with his spine.

"Let me *out*, motherfucker!" Mason shrieks, with a voice that could only come from a place as dark as those eyes.

Before, Dante felt in his heart that Mason might be possessed, but maybe there was a sliver of him that was a little naive and that things couldn't be as bad as they are. This morning, right now, his heart and mind are filled with certainty. That voice, like walking through glass barefoot as thunder crashes. The unnatural way that he moves like some kind of creature from the darkest corners of the mind. Those are enough to believe that demons are real.

Dante stands back, eyes held wide by fear. "What are you?" he asks. "You aren't Mason, what kind of demon are you?"

The boy groans as a smile creeps onto his face. "You mean you don't know?" He jerks forward, swiping at his father, snapping his jaw like a rabid animal. The chain stops him, keeping his reaching arm mere inches from Dante. "I am your undoing!" His wagging fingers curl into a fist as he pulls it into a defensive position. "You're going to die, Dante." His fist shakes like it's holding onto too much energy. "And then," Mason opens his hand and holds it still, "everyone around you will be better for it." He wiggles his fingers playfully as he cackles.

Dante rushes out of the basement to avoid further instigating from this monster. The laughter echoes at his back as he runs up the stairs. He knows what he needs to do now.

Chapter Twenty

With church starting in just twenty minutes, Dante is teetering on the edge of madness. His absence will raise concern, and people will be calling. Grace and Karl will wonder where Mason is. It will only get worse when those calls go to voicemail. He retrieves his phone from his bedroom and sees that there are already four missed calls, three of them from Susan and one from Grace. He begins playing the voice messages.

First message: Hey this is Susan, just checkin' on ya. If you're pickin' up the utensils for the luncheon I thought I told you I went ahead and got them anyway. See you soon, Mister Dante. Bye!

Next message: Hey, just checkin' in. Haven't heard from ya. People are starting to get in and I know you're normally here by now. At least that's what I thought, I was just checkin'. Take care, Bye!

Next message: Mister Dante, where are you? People are startin' to ask about you. What should I tell 'em? Are you on your way? Let me know, okay, bye!

Next message: Hey, Dante, um, it's Grace. Is everything alright? Susan is starting to be ... well ... Susan. She actually asked me to call you but, I–I don't know what to say. Can you please call her? Actually. This is unlike you. Call me and let me know you're okay, please.

"What's your plan, God? Everyone always talks about your plan," Dante says to the dead space in the dining room. "SHOW ME YOUR PLAN!" he cries.

"There is no plan!" Mason bellows from the basement. "God is up there laughing at you while He watches you suffer for His ... enjoyment."

Dante ignores the demon downstairs that continues to taunt him. *What are the odds? My son gets possessed by one of Satan's helpers and I'm supposed to be in church right now. Could the timing be any worse?*

He takes a seat at his computer where he is eyeing a Bible that he keeps nearby. The thought occurs that he should see what scripture has to say about eradicating evil and chasing off demonic forces. Leaning back in the chair he thumbs through page after page in search of one of the mentions of demon possession. He finds a passage—Matthew 8:28—that tells a story of two violent men that crossed paths with Jesus. The men asked if he had come to torture them before their appointed time.

Jesus was met with hostility from the two men, but they respected his power. Nearby were a herd of feeding pigs. The men had eventually begged Jesus, "If you drive us out, send us into the herd of pigs."

He said to them, "Go!" and the demons fled the bodies of the men and went into the pigs as the entire herd rushed away into the lake where they drowned.

Dante cannot help but to snicker, shaking his head as he closes the book. *Okay, I'm just going to go downstairs and tell the demon to go.* He sets the books back where he got it from and taps his keyboard to wake up his computer. *Well, I'm definitely no Jesus Christ. I can hardly get my son to listen without the demon in him lately.*

As he logs onto his computer he opens his Google Chrome browser. His fingers blaze along the keyboard, hoping for answers from the internet.

How to perform an exorcism is what he types into the search bar.

Right at the top of the results, Wikipedia, the all-knowing, second only to the one and only *true* God. The God that is not here at the moment. Of course, Wikipedia has developed quite the reputation for lacking credibility over the last couple decades, but blind faith charges forward with Dante behind the screen as he reads.

In the process of an exorcism the person possessed may be restrained so that they do not harm themselves or any person present. The exorcist then prays and commands for the demons to retreat. The Catholic priest recites certain prayers – the Lord's Prayer, Hail Mary, and the Athanasian Creed.

The good news, the 'demon' is restrained. The bad news, however, is that Dante is not a Catholic priest. He scrolls through the results, scouring site previews and similar suggested searches. He stops at a Quora.com link titled *Is there an easy way to perform an exorcism?*

Clicking the link, it offers many entries from regular people. Nothing produced on this site seems to be geared toward instructions on how to banish a demon from a possessed person. A majority of the entries just seem to be armchair experts just mimicking whatever magic and light show they've seen in the movies.

The next stop is Reddit. One person asks about how to perform an exorcism on himself. The comments are mostly unhelpful, and at times comical. Aside from the toxicity plastered all over the comment section, the few insightful responses suggest seeking a mental health professional, or contacting a Priest or Rabbi.

The one consistent thing mentioned is that to perform the ritual, it is imperative to have a relationship with God. Dante cringes at that sentiment knowing that he plays the part of pastor, but lately has felt his faith wane as he seeks guidance in his own life.

Back to Google, he types *what items are needed to perform an exorcism?* The University of Oregon has an article that suggests the following: *Sacred objects used in exorcisms include holy water, crucifixes, candles, incense, holy scrolls or tablets, oil for anointing, holy swords, prayer books, and relics of the deity. These objects are believed to overpower and weaken the demon.*

Dante jots the list of items down on a post-it note and opens a new tab on the browser. *How to perform an exorcism yourself.* More muddy and unreliable results, until he sees one that catches his eye. *Do-It-Yourself Exorcism.* He clicks the link in a hurry. The website isn't one he has heard of but seems well-built and looks spiffy enough. *DRIVE OUT DEMONS IN JUST A FEW EASY STEPS* it says across the top of the website in a playful cursive.

He scrolls past headers that offer the definition of possession, the authorities, and also why anyone can do it, so long as they believe in Jesus Christ. He arrives near the middle of the page, where the simple steps are laid out, made to look as simple as following a baking recipe.

Step 1. Make sure the possessed person is restrained, to avoid injury to anyone within reach.

Step 2. Be bold. Be confident.

Step 3. Call the Demon by name (if you know it).

Step 4. Cast out all evil spirits in the name of Jesus Christ.

Easy peasy, Dante thinks, knowing that it can't possibly be that easy. He opens another tab. *How to contact the Catholic church about an exorcism.* As he is reading about who to contact and the process involved in enlisting help from an exorcist, there is a banging from the basement. The chain rattles and the pipe screams from the metal cuff scraping along. Screeching rings out and the sound is so abrasive Dante involuntarily covers his ears.

"Oh, holy man!" the unnaturally deep voice taunts. "You're wasting time up there. Why don't you come and let me out, and we can go look for your boy together."

Dante pulls out his phone. More missed calls. Church started fifteen minutes ago and he isn't there. He goes into his contacts and dials Dr. Bryant. The phone rings, but he knows that his therapist isn't likely to take calls from patients on Sunday morning. He gets the voicemail greeting and stands, the chair legs violating the floor with a dry squeal as it's pushed back. He paces the dining room and kitchen with the phone to one ear and a finger plugging the other, as Mason's demon is still sliding the cuffs across the piping as loud as possible.

Please leave a message after the beep.

"Yeah, I'm not sure what's going on. I'm ... I'm sorry to be calling this early ... oh, this is Dante Mitchell by the way," his words fall out of his mouth like a bad juggler performing. "Listen, I need to talk to you. As soon as possible, if you can. I might have done something, or–" He groans, pacing around the dinner table. "I don't know, maybe something happened and ... I don't know who else to turn to," Dante sighs. "This was stupid. I'm sorry. I shouldn't have bothered you. Have a good weekend. I'll just see you next week."

Dante hangs up after that erratic spewing of words with no direction. He sits back in front of the computer. His phone rings, vibrating on the desktop as he faces the screen down. With his nose back to his research he toggles back onto the tab with the website with the easy steps. As he scrolls farther down he sees *Read My Story Here* as a link. He clicks it and discovers it is from the creator of the website.

The summary of the article is that the guy is living in an apartment and notices his roommate exhibiting signs of possession. The symptoms are all listed out, and Dante's intrigue is only overcome by the fear for his boy when he sees that this itemized list aligns almost exactly like what is happening with Mason. The situation went from bad to worse in a hurry, the article says. The guy reached out to the Catholic church initially when he had his own suspicions of possession. Despite his naivety, he still reached out and when he spoke with a so-called expert, he was quickly dismissed and told to first contact a mental health professional and take steps to have his roommate professionally evaluated. If they deemed it credible he would be committed and held for observation for at least ten days.

The thought of having Mason taken away and locked in a psychiatric institute is unsettling. His stomach climbs up his throat at the idea of having to regularly visit his son in a mental ward. Dante thinks about a time when Mason was crying in his arms and he was able to simply hold him close to his chest and walk with him while he rubbed his back to calm him. The room feels cold as he considers how far from that moment they are. Exploring hypothetical psychiatric treatment options feels colder.

The arguments and reactions from Grace are not something he looks forward to, should he go this route. Continuing with the article, the guy lists off the steps mentioned at the previous page and cites that these steps were successful with his roommate and that they will work if there is a need for an emergency exorcism.

Scribbling quickly, Dante has the steps to cleansing the spirit from the affected person. Determined not to lose his boy, he will do anything to make things right. Maintaining everything else is another story.

Chapter Twenty-One

With a couple of prayers already in mind, Dante begins scrambling about the house, grabbing all of the necessary items that the internet told him he will need. After rifling through cabinets in the kitchen, he settles on a stainless steel mixing bowl that he hasn't used since Grace left. He holds it under the sink faucet until it is filled about halfway. "Lord, God Almighty, creator of all life, of body and soul, we ask you to bless this water, as we use it in faith. Forgive our sins and save us from all illness and the power of evil." He moves his hand over the water, pantomiming a cross. Holy water has been acquired.

He goes upstairs and grabs an old wooden cross from the top drawer of his bedside table. It belonged to his dad and it used to hang on the wall of the home he grew up in. On the top shelf of a bookcase in his bedroom, he pulls down his family Bible. Worn and aged, it has a soft cover and gold edges.

Rushing back downstairs, he grabs the table salt and bowl of water. Cross and salt in his pocket, Bible under his arm, and bowl in his hands. "Mason?" he calls down, gently.

He hears no response as he steadies himself with each step. "Mason?" he says again, less gentle than before, continuing down the stairs with the water sloshing in the bowl.

No response.

As Dante's feet hit the chilled floor, he sees Mason, standing with his back to him, arm pulled over his head looking like he is hanging, mid-spin from the rim after a slam dunk. As Dante maintains a safe distance, staying close to the opposite wall, Mason moves subtly, keeping his back to him.

"What are you doing there, son?"

Mason's arm fidgets and twitches in sync with his leg. Knees contracting enough to cause his body to jolt while he stands. It's like he has a limp without taking any steps. Dante sets the bowl onto the floor and the Bible there beside it, and he crosses the room to have a better look at what Mason is doing.

With an audible gasp that is quickly hushed by Dante's hands, he isn't able to cover his frightened eyes as he sees what is happening. Mason turns his head, looking at Dante over his shoulder, as he is digging a fork into his thigh. The same one Dante left within reach when he fled before.

"Mason," Dante pleads. "Put the ... put the fork down."

Mason growls, deep from his belly, turning his attention back to his thigh as he continues to ignore his father.

Dante fights back the impulse to hack up the rushed breakfast he ate earlier after seeing the amount of blood that has poured down Mason's leg. Spatters of blood pepper the wall and floor and shine against the aluminum finish on parts of the furnace. The sound of the fork moving through the skin and fatty tissue raises the hair on Dante's neck.

"Son ... Mason," he says, taking a step closer with his hands in a defensive position. "You've gotta put the fork down, let me have the fork, you're going to hurt yourself, seriously."

Mason turns his back to him once more, grumbling, but still digging in and twitching.

Dante turns and looks at the Bible and the bowl of holy water on the floor. He reaches into his pocket and pulls out the salt shaker and the cross. "I need to do something, Mason," he says, holding out the cross with unsteady hands. "I don't think you're going to like it." He begins to draw a line of salt on the floor between him and Mason, with eyes locked onto Mason's back. "Just remember, your dad loves you," he says, choked up as his words tumble off of his frightened tongue. "I'm just doing what I think is best."

Dante wields the wooden cross like a dagger. He sidesteps to the bowl of blessed water and dips his fingertips in. "Our Father, who art in heaven," he begins flicking water at Mason's back, "hallowed be thy name."

Mason immediately screams, jerking his face to the ceiling as his hands cover his ears. "Silence!" he cries as the fork bounces onto the floor, the tines painted with red. Dante is able to reach with his foot and kicks the fork away, similar to how a police officer would do to a criminal with a weapon.

Dante continues to splash the Mason-dressed demon. "Thy kingdom come, thy will be done," he recites, only to agitate the imprisoned boy. Like an explosion, Mason lurches toward his father, only stopping to acknowledge the salt barrier on the floor. Dante stumbles back. "On earth as it is ..."

Mason's eyes pull away from the line in front of him and land on Dante, who has stopped the prayer to watch in awe of the demon. Mason smiles, his lips thinning as it stretches so wide that it no longer looks like Mason. He takes his free hand and licks his two fingers before quickly plunging them into the wound on his leg with no reaction to any pain at all. His fingers slide out and he points at Dante with bloody fingers. The two standoff for only a few seconds as Mason flicks the blood at Dante's face and then brushes the salt away with his foot, undeterred by it.

Shaken up, and struggling to pace backwards, Dante begins to say the prayer once more as he tries to remember the instructions. *Step 2. Be bold, be confident,* although he realizes that his fear is evident in his voice. He splashes more water directly into Mason's face, right as the boy is brought to a stop by the outstretched chain.

Mason leers at the chain, growling from his belly like kindling cracking in a fire. Those deep and dark eyes turn to Dante. "Don't you have someplace to be ... Daddy?"

Ignoring the question, Dante tries to stand firm, continuing the prayer, raising his voice as he splashes more water at the beast while keeping a safe distance to avoid any sudden swings that Mason might take. Mason roars and raises his hand and all of the junk that was sent flying across the basement before is flying across to the other side. Projectiles slam against the wall, crashing into the washer and dryer. A basket clips Dante's hands, knocking the cross free. It hits the floor and Dante accidentally kicks over the bowl of water, causing most of it to spill onto the cold cement.

Mason reaches down, barely within reach and takes the cross. Dante scuffles to the stairs and turns back to see Mason drink what is left of the water in one gulp. Mason flings the bowl crashing loud into the wall. The surprise that grips Dante sends him rushing up the steps once more. *Why isn't holy water working?*

"I feel ... refreshed," Mason snarls. "Nothing is as satisfying as heaven on my tongue."

Chapter Twenty-Two

Hours later, Dante is sitting at the computer in his dining room once again. Perplexed by what ails his boy, yet determined to find a means to correct it, Dante spends more time researching some of the links he likely passed over before. Whatever attempt at an exorcism that was, was anything but productive.

What to do if an exorcism doesn't work?

What is the correct way to bless holy water?

Upon reading the many different passages online about performing exorcisms yourself, Dante has noticed one recurring theme in most of these articles. One that gives him cause for concern if he's being honest with himself. Traditionally, an exorcist is Catholic and their presence is approved by the church beforehand. Some things contradict the traditional ideology by suggesting that performing an exorcism doesn't have to be a Catholic thing exclusively, and that so long as the person performing is born-again or carries a deep belief and devotion to the Lord in his heart.

Dante has questioned his belief more and more lately, all while doing the Lord's work in his community. He has felt his faith wavering for longer than he is willing to admit to himself, only until now. It started when his father passed away and the world was left on his shoulders to carry. Any plans he had to carve out his own identity were brought to a screeching halt in the name of God, and that may have stirred up some unspoken resentment. Once a divorce was thrown in the mix, depression seeped in wearing a coat made of self doubt and it smothered any dreams he may have once had.

This will be a problem, he thinks. His faith is a broken soul on wobbly legs at best, and for more than a year he has gotten by being able to smile and just dress nicely. *Is it a sin to still call yourself a pastor if your belief is fading?* If it is, he will have to make it work to save his son. The alternative is asking for help and showcasing what happened here. Explaining this would sound crazy and if this is the only way, then he just prays that God isn't punishing him. The guilt is like a dog gnawing on a bone in his mind as his fingers dance on the keys, desperate to find some new piece of information that offers hope. Just a crumb to be led in the right direction would be pivotal.

Landing on what feels like the millionth article from an archdiocese website, he finds the words running together. He reads what's on the screen, but his brain is somewhere else. Somewhere far far away. The words enter his brain as he reads the mush of letters, but the information is overshadowed by the voices of people he knows. Voices from people who are supposed to love him. People who are supposed to support him. Voices he recalls validating every insecurity he has in his heart.

His father's booming voice echoes in his brain, as it was from the basement. *You're gonna let all of these people down too. Just like you're lettin' ya son down.*

Words spoken from the mouth of his son, but the voice of his father, used with intent to cut deep. *Maybe he was right*, Dante wonders, continuing to read empty words. Dante is beginning to feel like the disappointment that his father's voice said he is. It was bad enough he felt like he was letting God down already, in his own private thoughts, but to hear it out loud only makes him sink lower.

The behavior from Mason recently hasn't helped at all either. *Since when does Mason seek to be combative and rebellious?* The words from Mason that break his heart, the attacks that break his flesh, and now the evil presence handcuffed downstairs with no clear answer on how to break.

Even at church, overhearing Susan outside of his office. *Dante is a nice guy, but he isn't his dad,* she said. *If this woman who is there to assist me is talking this way and feels this way, what is she not saying? How does she really feel?* It might be safe to assume that others probably feel this way too. Everyone else has good intentions and are hoping for the best while Dante wades through the mess that his life is becoming.

Dante's thoughts are broken by the vibration of his phone, rattling across the desktop. His eyes break from the screen and he realizes that he just read a bunch of words, but absorbed none of them. He grabs the phone, leaning back in the chair as he looks at the notifications on his screen. Twelve missed calls, twenty-six unread text messages, and some comments on his last Youtube video. He puts the phone face down on the desk, leans back into the computer and opens a new tab for Youtube.

The little bell icon at the top right corner of the webpage shows several notifications. He clicks there to see a few comments on his last video.

What's going on with you?

Everything okay?

Where r u @?

U still cumin to the lunchin?

God bless you and your family.

Hey man, we missed you today. Susan's husband stepped in and said some nice things and read from the book but everyone could tell he was just making it up as he went. Hope to see you next week!

The luncheon is going on still, assuming that someone is handling it all. The shame he feels knowing that people are disappointed in him not being there, and their worry, only piles onto the guilt he is already feeling. He leans back in the chair, staring at the screen. Comments from people he knows in real life reaching out. *How much of that is because they care? How much of that is just so they can get the scoop and gossip about it?* The silence of the house creates a ringing in his ears along with the soft hum from the computer. The morning is lost but there is a future to be salvaged, but he just can't figure out how to do it without consequences. The optics of this won't be understood no matter how passionately he explains it.

His head throbs; a headache is slithering in to pulsate with subtle pains that keep his focus off-balance. He closes his eyes and there is immediate relief from the bright white LED screen feeding his brain. Dante knows he needs a plan, but the pieces aren't fitting to this puzzle and at some point he will need to– knuckles rapping on the glass to the front door interrupt the deep thinking.

"Oh no," Dante murmurs.

Chapter Twenty-Three

The knock sends panic through Dante's body like a shock of electricity. He stands so fast the computer chair rolls back a few feet.

Knuckles rattle the glass with the same rhythm as before while Dante cowers, hoping not to be seen somehow. *Pretend we're not home*, he thinks.

"Dante, are you there?" Grace asks. "Mason?" She knocks on the solid part of the door, this time a little harder, turning the open space inside into a bass drum.

Dante huffs, sneaking away from the computer to hide behind the kitchen counter. The shape of Grace moves around on the front porch, as Dante can see through the thin curtains that cover the window. *Maybe she will just go away.*

"Dante," she shouts. "This isn't like you. Everybody is freaking out." She shields her eyes and presses her face to the glass as if to be able to see through the curtain. "And I'm a little worried too." She goes back to knocking. *Boom boom boom boom boom* all through the house.

He winces at each bang, unsure what his next move is.

"Just go away, just go away, just go," he begs under his breath.

"Ok ... I'm gonna use my spare key ... I'm coming in."

No! He had forgotten that she still has a key, in case of emergencies. He springs from his crouched position and races to the door.

He hears her keys jingling just before the door knob swallows the key and the tumblers that grind within the lock begin to turn. The knob twists and the door eases open with Grace's face peaking through.

Dante rushes to the door and throws a hand against it to keep her from entering. "Hey, what are you doing here?" he asks with a forced positivity in his voice.

Grace jumps, startled. She yelps with a hand slapping against her heart as she steps back.

"Sorry, sorry, sorry. I didn't mean to–"

"Dante. What the– what is going on?" she asks.

"What do you mean?" he responds, as if everything is perfectly normal.

"Um, I've been calling you. I've been texting you. I want to know that you are okay. I want to know that my *son* is okay."

Dante looks behind him, keeping his body between the cracked door opening and the inside of the house.

"I know other people have tried calling you and you're not answering your phone and this is–"

"Alright, alright, listen everything is fine. We're just–"

"Oh my God!" she blurts out, squinting her eyes to study Dante's face. "Is that ... is that blood?"

He turns his face to the glass in the door and sees his reflection. Specks of blood litter his face. The heightened sense of awareness is piloting his body apparently, because anything he does or says is suspicious now. *No one can know what is really going on. Not until I can fix it. Don't lie to her.* "Yes." *But don't tell her the truth either.* "It's nothing to worry about."

Grace's mouth hangs agape. "My ex-husband has my son, has dropped off the face of the planet, and has blood all over his face. And I'm not supposed to worry?" she grills him.

Dante lets out a tired sigh. "No. I've just felt sick. Since last night. I was trying to rest. I might have thrown up a few–"

"Why couldn't you at least return a call or text?"

"I'm sorry, I just," he starts, unable to finish the thought. His eyes avoid her like a puppy that's been shamed after peeing in the house.

"You look like a car hit you, Dante." The silence hangs for a moment. "I'm worried about you."

Dante wedges himself between the open door and the frame, staring into the sky, or the house across the street, or anywhere that means he doesn't have to look her in the face and feel her familiar judging gaze burning through him. "I'm just not doing too good is all."

Frustrated, she crosses her arms, leaning with a cocked hip. "You need to start taking care of yourself Dante. I know things are hard for you, but you need to figure your shit out."

"I'm working on it!" he snaps. He stares at her, a little shocked that she cursed. He hasn't heard her curse in a while. Another awkward pause as he blocks the doorway.

She sighs. "Where is Mason? I wanna see him before I leave." She tries to go into the house, attempting to squeeze past Dante but he pulls the door closed more and holds his hand out.

"Stop!" he says, very assertive. "Listen, everything is fine. I'm telling you," he speaks slowly, and enunciates each word clearly. "I haven't touched my phone because I don't feel well. I am trying to–"

"Oh, come on, Dante, that's bullshit. You know it. I know it. Since when do you miss church? You were sick, but you didn't make arrangements? Or tell anybody? That is not like you at all."

"So, what? I'm not allowed to be sick!?"

"No! I'm just–" Grace steps back and takes a deep breath, resting her finger and thumb on the bridge of her nose. "The whole reason we stopped working, the whole reason I left ..." she starts, fighting back tears as her voice betrays her, "is because you always put work first. What is different? You really don't see why this is so bizarre?" She stares at him, dumbfounded. "I want to take Mason with me."

Dante shakes his head. "No Grace. You're not taking Mason. It is my time with him."

"You're not well, Dante! Fucking look at yourself!" she shouts over him. The former couple argue, talking over one another, tit for tat.

"I'm not going to keep going around in circles with you right here where everyone can hear us like it's Jerry Springer!"

"I want to see Mason, go and tell him I want to see him."

"I'm not doing anything. You just showed up here! You can come by tomorrow–"

"I just showed up here because you didn't answer your phone! I want my son!"

"*Our* son!" he yells. "*Our son!* I'm completely capable of spending time with *our* son, Grace!"

"I'm just asking to see him! Why is that such a problem!?"

The headache returns as Dante's vision turns fuzzy. The colors bleed together and the noises sound like they're all underwater. Blood pumps aggressively in his head and he closes his eyes and concentrates on the blood pumping. The rhythm of the pulsation, pounding and pounding as Grace continues to pound and pound away at him with her words. This impossible situation is only being made more complicated and increasing the risk to Mason and himself the longer she stands on the porch screaming at him. The drowning noises and focused sound of his blood pumping become one sound. One sound until his eyes open and the world rushes back to him in clear vision, vivid colors, and clean noises.

"You need to leave now," Dante says, lowering his voice. His eyes are no longer avoiding hers. "You can call tonight." Dante removes the spare key from the lock and shoves it into his pocket as Grace watches with her jaw hanging open. "You can come by tomorrow. But I am his father. I will take care of this. Have a good day, Grace." Dante backs into the house and closes the door on the conversation.

Grace lingers on the porch for a minute as Dante has a seat on the bottom step. "You better answer your phone when I call!" she yells as she taps her fingernail on the window in the door before disappearing from the porch. Relief washes over Dante as he listens to her footfalls against each step outside.

Chapter Twenty-Four

P acing the living room with his hands on his head, fingers interlocked, Dante is distracted with the tall task of trying not to hyperventilate. The tension just a moment ago with Grace was too much. He recognizes that he had to lie and say anything to get out of that situation. Grace knowing what is happening right now is not an option and her coming in or seeing Mason puts their family at risk. "She's going to come back, she's going to be calling, I don't know what to do," he mutters to himself.

The next move is a guessing game at this stage, and any sense of a plan there might have been, is long gone. Dante sits at the dining room table. His leg bounces so hard and fast that the floor is shaking enough to rattle the picture frames on the walls. He picks at his cuticle on his thumb with his teeth as he stresses out over what to do next.

"Dad," Mason calls, sounding like his normal and sweet self. "Dad ... are you there?"

Dante stares into the dark doorway from where his son's voice echoes with the question. He hesitates to respond as his cuticle begins to bleed between his front teeth.

"Was that my mom I heard?" Mason asks, with concern gripping his words. "Is she here? ... Mom!?"

Dante's eyes tighten, like closed shutters on a storefront. Tears build in the corners of his eyes. "Yeah ... that was your mom."

"Where is she?"

"She had to leave." Dante opens his eyes and goes to the top of the steps. "I'll be taking you home soon though. You can see your mom really soon, buddy."

The chain to the handcuffs clink gently as Mason leans into the light hitting the floor from the open doorway. "Can you just drive me there right now, Dad?"

Mason stands there, afraid, dirty, and bloody, straining his neck to look at his father, blocking the light upstairs. Dante walks down and stands in front of his boy. Vulnerable and famished, Dante's heart breaks to see him this way. His lips quiver, not allowing words to form. Mason backs away, loosening the tension on the chain. "I'm so sorry, son." Dante closes the distance between them and pulls Mason in a close embrace. The floodgates open and the tears flow freely. Mason wraps his arms around his father as well and he also begins to cry.

Dante holds Mason's head close to his heart, with a tender hand on his cheek. "I love you so much. I never imagined anything like this ever. Please, just tell me how to get us out of this," he asks as more of a general question to the universe.

Mason's whimpers escape into his dad's chest. "I don't know ... you could just let me go."

Dante pulls away, his hands cradling Mason's face. "I want to ... I really do," he says, frantically. "You understand that when I let you out of here, no one can ever know, right?"

"Yeah."

"Nobody!" Dante shouts. "Not even your mother."

Mason stares back, tear streaks clearing the grime from his face. The eyes glisten and the crying unleashes. The sound of Mason's pain and need for someone to save him tears through Dante, unable to do that. The shame that overcomes Dante makes the wails from his son impossible to endure. He backs away and crouches by the stairs, sealing his ears with his forearms to block out the pained cries of someone who loves him and needs him more than anything.

The covered ears only dampen the noise, as the sound still seeps into his ear canals, slithers to his brain, and wrenches on his heart more with each beat. Those cries become something else in the attempt to not hear them. Dante raises his head to see Mason standing. With a face wearing no expression, the sound of the crying continues, like surround-sound in Dante's head. "Make it stop!" he shouts.

Mason's head dips to the side as his eyes subtly become the deep black orbs that signify that the evil isn't finished and something else is still driving his son's body like a vehicle for agony. Dante's confusion is not difficult to read. The crying continues, sounding less natural with each second. More like a record skipping in his brain as the pitch falls slowly, descending into a hollow and deep decibel often associated with the sounds of evil.

"Your wife, Grace ... she needed you," Mason's voice rings out, but his lips do not move. "When she was devoted to you, wholeheartedly, you chose time and time again to put others ahead of her. You were so busy trying to look good for others when you should've been being good to your wife ... she only needed you to be one thing ... a husband."

Dante shuffles back, slowly up the steps as his son's black eyes chill his blood. Dante lands in the kitchen, a broken man with a situation that is seeming impossible to repair with each passing moment.

Dante stands at the stove. The flame under the skillet helps to create the pancakes that he will have for dinner and serve to Mason. The other day he asked for pancakes shaped like a dog and now that seems like the least he can do for his son, all things considered. He uses a cookie cutter that Grace left behind to cut the shapes. Dante tosses the outside of the cookie cutter onto his plate, and adds the dog-shaped pancake onto others that are stacked on a paper towel.

Dante scarfs down his food while standing at the counter. The dog-shaped pancakes are still warm and Dante carries them downstairs with a bottle of cold water. Mason is sitting on the floor, quiet, drawing circles on his bent knee with his finger. Dante sets the napkin onto the floor and the water beside it. This time, there is no plate, no silverware, and not even any syrup. "Here you are, son, I figure you might be hungry."

Mason stares at the food, breathing out from his nose loudly. "I really have to pee, dad."

Another element to this arrest that Dante failed to consider. "One second."

Dante scurries up the stairs and begins rummaging through the cabinet under the kitchen sink. He grabs a cleaning bucket, removes the supplies from it and sets them on the floor. He heads back downstairs with the handles in his hand and presents it to Mason like the perfect answer to a riddle.

Crisis averted.

Mason stands and scowls at the bucket, then looks at Dante, holding eye contact as he pisses himself where he stands. The urine overtakes the mildew-ey smell immediately as the stream runs down his leg and pools around Mason's feet. Dante leaves the bucket on the floor and goes back upstairs.

CHAPTER TWENTY-FIVE

MONDAY

Monday morning arrives and Dante awakes on the couch where he must have zonked out last night. His sore and tired body cracks and pops as he raises up with his messy hair. His eyes squint to ward off the bright morning sunshine that creeps through the closed blinds. He reaches for his phone on the coffee table and the screen lights up. Thirty-eight missed calls, sixty unread text messages, nineteen new voicemails, and an overwhelming amount of Facebook, Instagram, and YouTube notifications.

He scrolls through the text messages and sees that most of the messages are from the same people. Without even reading them, he clears the notifications. He clears the call notifications and the social media pings but as he is scrolling through the new voicemails he sees that his therapist, Dr. Bryant left one, less than an hour ago. He stands up and yawns, stretching as he plays the voicemail from Dr. Bryant.

Dante, Dr. Bryant here, you sounded a bit stressed in your message you left yesterday, I wanted to follow up and make sure you're doing okay. I've gotta be honest with you, it kind of scared me. I'm concerned now. Call me back, let's meet today if you're available. Talk to you soon, bye.

He goes about his morning getting himself cleaned up, as he realizes he hasn't showered in days and has worn the same filthy shirt since Saturday. Mason is hollering from the basement but Dante is on the second floor, with the bathroom door shut. The hot water runs as the fresh razor runs underneath the stream before Dante takes off his five o'clock shadow, one stroke at a time between several rinses.

He gets dressed, opting for a basic pair of jeans, and a plain black t-shirt. Monday begins and he knows he normally has things to tend to at church but he tries to not think about that. More pressing concerns hold his attention and there is no better time to meditate than right now. Clearing his mind might allow him to see a clear path to saving his son and his reputation, or so he hopes.

As he sits on his pillow on the floor of his bedroom he looks at his phone before setting it away. Checking notifications, being selective, he sees people asking where he is, asking why there was no daily prayer video this morning, and other things of that sort. People must see that he is active online because he receives direct messages from several people all at once before closing the apps entirely.

He tosses the phone away and begins his meditation with hopes of enlightenment and a positive attitude afterward. It is a brand new day and he is thankful to see it. *The only way to go from here is up,* he thinks to himself as he closes his eyes and begins his breathing routine.

Chapter Twenty-Six

Through the morning and into the afternoon Dante has spent his time satisfying the minor chores around the house. Mason and him ate toast for breakfast this morning and now Dante is realizing that he may need some things around the house, and soon. Groceries are running low and he has noticed some essentials in need of restocking as well. The thought of running out to the grocery, if only for thirty minutes, crosses his mind but the chance of someone seeing him is too great to risk. This small town is filled with kind souls and chatty tongues, none of them strangers. Even more nerve-racking is the possibility that Mason is home alone and something happens.

With anxiety driving Dante's feet, he parades back and forth between the living room and the dining area. The situation is bad now but Dante is considering just how bad things might get if he doesn't figure something out soon. *At what point do I swallow my pride and face the music to protect my son? Is this life that only burdens me worth safeguarding?* The mental gymnastics and weight of the circumstances have nearly pushed him to the point of taking the risk, and maybe even calling Grace, and telling her everything.

And that's when there is a knock at the door.

Frozen in place, the rational thoughts of a desperate man flee from his mind as the panic rushes in. Mason begins to cry out from below after the knock.

"Hello!?" he shouts. "Down here! Help me!" Mason sounds like he is in trouble, in the way that a hostage might sound.

Dante tiptoes quickly to the top of the steps. "Shhhh," he tells his son. "You have to keep it down. If anyone hears you I won't be able to help you," he reminds him as he shuts the basement door, muffling the sudden cries for help, but not completely silencing them.

Ducked behind the kitchen counter, Dante's eyes scan the windows beside the front door. He can make out the shadow and shape of the person. Tall, likely a man, and someone who has their hands and face pressed against the glass as if to see through the curtain if they focus enough. The shadowed man on the porch knocks again, his knuckles rapping against the glass. "Helloooo?" He knocks again, this time with a musical number like you would use for a secret knock. The silhouette disappears from sight and Dante scuttles over toward the front door, hunched over in his movement.

He studies the window before getting too close, ensuring that no one is still hanging out on the porch. Certain that no one is there, Dante peeks out of the corner of the window, moving the curtain slightly to get a view of the street. Dante lets go of the curtain and hangs his head as he blows out a held breath. Karl's big yellow Jeep sits in the driveway, blocking Dante in if he wants to go anywhere. Dante stands, still tiptoeing back toward the kitchen when he sees the shadow peering through the kitchen window over the sink. The curtain isn't low enough to hide him from being seen and he locks eyes with his ex-wife's new boyfriend.

Busted.

Dante straightens himself to stand upright and smiles as he raises his hand. Karl uses a hand motion, signaling that he is coming around to the front. Behind the protection of a fraudulent smile, Dante stands while Mason continues to holler downstairs. "It's okay, everything is fine, if I just see what he wants and get him to leave, we'll be fine. Everything is fine," Dante murmurs to himself just loud enough to not hear his racing heart beating in his ears.

The front door opens and Karl is standing there waiting. He knows something, his eyes look over and past Dante. "Hey Karl, what brings you around here?" he asks in his best attempt to not sound like he is holding his son captive downstairs in the dark.

"Hey, I'm looking for Grace. Is she in there?"

Dante shakes his head left to right, lips stretching thin to appear confused. "Noooo, she texted me that–"

"I know she's here, she called me before to tell me she was coming over and I haven't heard from her since yesterday. I can see her–"

"She isn't here," Dante interrupts, matching Karl's aggressive tone. "I can tell her you stopped by if I hear from her."

Karl stares at Dante, still, like an animal does before pouncing. "She mentioned she was worried and wanted to check on you and Mason."

"I spoke to her already," Dante lies. "Everything is fine. She was just–"

"Where is Mason?" Karl asks, sizing up Dante on his doorstep. Karl's eyes investigating Dante's appearance and the house.

"*My son,*" Dante snaps, "is in his room."

During a brief pause, Mason screams and Karl's face lights up in response. "Mason!" Karl shouts, using his size to shove past Dante into the house. Dante stumbles to the side, nearly tumbling over his own feet as Karl marches through the living room. "Mason! ... Where ya at?"

"Help me! Please!" The yelling comes from the basement. "Down here!" Karl's head pivots quickly to the closed basement door.

He opens the door, standing atop the steps, looking down at a grimey and handcuffed Mason. "What in the fuck?" he mutters to himself, feeling his skin crawl and his mouth dry as the horror saps him of all anger and fills him with dread. He turns away and before he can muster the words to confront Dante he is met with a wooden kitchen stool to the head that sends him spilling down the steps. As his body bangs on every step on the way down, crashing onto the unforgiving concrete below, Dante watches from the top step, dropping the stool with fire in his eyes.

"Why couldn't you just go!? I didn't answer for a reason, you should've just gone!" Dante screams into the echoing dungeon. Rivulets of sweat run down his reddened face as he runs down the stairs.

Karl groans, holding his head, desperate to get back to his feet. He falls sideways, immediately bouncing off the wall before noticing Dante standing right in his face.

Dante grabs the front of Karl's shirt but is met with resistance. The two men scuffle but it only lasts for a moment before Dante shoves the already stunned Karl against the wall. His skull hits so hard that the back of his head bounces off the brick and his arms loosen up and fall to his side. Adrenaline tears through Dante, unwilling to let Karl ruin how he is handling the Mason situation. Another shove into the wall sends his head pinging again, making a nasty smack sound of flesh on stone that leaves a red splotch on the wall. Another knock into the wall smears the blood, and a fourth, and a fifth hit leaves new spots, each time brighter than the last. Karl's body slumps from Dante's grasp, despite the rage fueling him to continue shoving his head into the wall for a sixth and seventh time with his primal screaming.

With tense muscles and shaky exasperation, Dante lets go of Karl allowing him to fall to the floor, where he lies motionless. Blood pools around his head on the cold concrete as Dante stands there, wheezing with every breath as his chest rises and falls dramatically.

He backs away from Karl's body and looks over at Mason, who looks just as mortified as Dante, sobbing loud and involuntary with his body as far away from his father as the handcuffs will allow. His body trembles and Dante breaks right there as he looks at his son.

"Oh God, what've I done?" Dante erupts, walking over to his son. Mason resists and tenses up and turns his head away, whimpering into the shadows. "Listen," Dante says as he steps back to avoid scaring the boy any more than he already is. "I couldn't let him leave. He would have ruined everything." Abandoning the considerate nature, Dante approaches his son, grabbing his unsecured arm, pulling him to look him eye to eye. "I know that I shouldn't have you chained up down here like some sort of pet or something." Tears fill his eyes and words hang in his throat. "I'm trying to fix this. I need you to not have that … " he looks Mason up and down, "*evil* inside of you before I can let you out of here." Mason stares back, bottom lip puckered with puffy cheeks. "You understand why I have to figure this out right? People will think I'm crazy. They'll take you from me. Your mother will take you away. This whole town … they aren't going to understand, they'll just hear the headlines and finish the story before I can tell our side."

Dante lets Mason go and stands back up, walking over to Karl. "I never meant for this to happen," he says, nudging Karl's shoulder with his foot. He looks around the room, gesturing at the handcuffs with his hand. "I never meant for any of this to happen … we can still fix this."

Mason stares at his father through watery eyes. "I want my mommy."

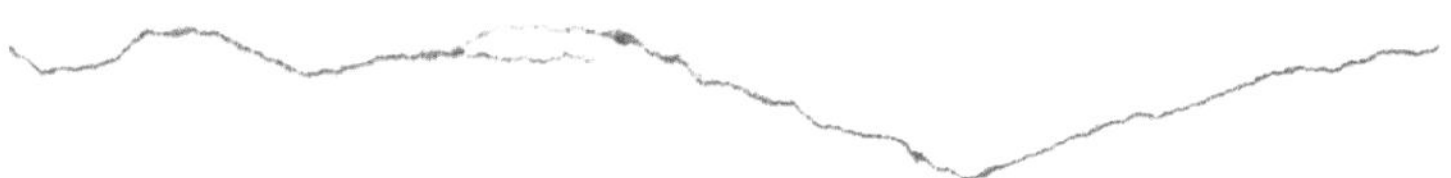

"Oh my God," Dante mutters. He leans over the bathroom sink as the faucet runs with hot steam rising to his battered reflection in the mirror. "What have I done, what have I done?" he repeats. His fist bangs on the side of the sink vanity as the cup with two toothbrushes rattles against the ceramic countertop. Inconsistent air patterns flow through his nose as the tears come. He faces his reflection with every bit of mental fatigue wearing on his physical face. His eyes carry bags beneath and the redness accompanies the look.

"Forgive me. Please!" he begs, breaking his eyes away from his reflection that stares back at him.

Dante feels the shame.

The guilt.

That mirror only casts his own judgment back at him.

"I didn't mean to do that! I know I didn't like the guy, but ..." Dante pounds his fist on the countertop again, repeatedly until the toothbrush cup falls over the edge and onto the floor and the underside of his closed fist goes numb. He ignores the mess. The weight of the body in his basement creates one more big problem in addition to Mason's affliction. As if things weren't stressful enough, the world is crumbling beneath Dante's feet as he tries to stay grounded.

Dante stares into the running stream of hot water as it flows into the drain. *People kill people all the time. Every day. Courts don't always judge murderers as awful people. Maybe someone will understand.* The water running isn't loud enough to muffle Dante's thoughts. *Or, maybe they won't understand.* He begins to cry hard. Sobbing uncontrollably.

"Karl didn't deserve that ... no one deserves that."

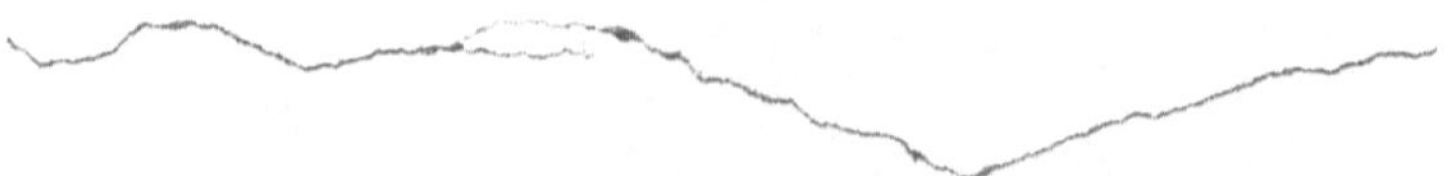

Mason stays quiet as a mouse for the remainder of the day. Dante does well to maintain the same operation he has kept up for the last three days. Empty Mason's bucket, feed him and bring him water, and pace the house nervously until God tears open the roof of his beautiful home and smites him on the spot for letting his faith waver for so long. The overactive imagination and anxiety only fuels thoughts of scenarios that are highly unlikely and in most cases impossible. Dante spends much of the day waiting for the hammer to fall and tending to Mason, anticipating another outburst or another display of demonic possession but it doesn't happen. The day is calm with exception to his actions throughout the house.

Dante takes notice in the afternoon of just how quiet and calm the house is. The peacefulness in the home makes it hard for him not to think about how big the house is for just him (and sometimes Mason) ever since Grace moved out. The thought of selling the home is still too much for his heart and mind to take but he can't help but think about how this really is *too much* house for one man.

The sun goes down and Dante tries to speak to Mason before bed. His son is unresponsive and refuses to speak. Meditation before bed happens, but it is done poorly, as the thoughts that enter his mind aren't exhaled away as easily, but rather latch onto him like a grocery bag caught in the wind against a chain link fence. He gives up after ten minutes of seeing Grace's face when she last yelled at him. He sees Karl's face when he looked at him completely horrified before plummeting into the basement. He sees the pain plastered on his son's face after witnessing everything. *This is what guilt must look like.* The day lingers and settles in his skin and he just wants to sleep. *Tomorrow will be a better day.*

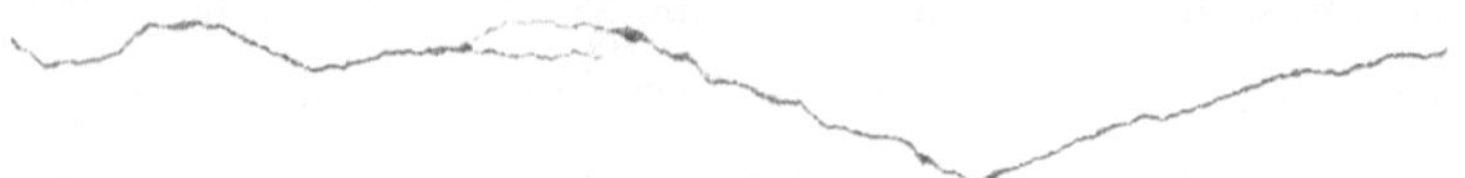

Dante and Grace stand outside on the porch. The scene feels familiar to Dante as the two have conversations that become arguments
and circle round and round like the same chase they've done for the
last year and a half. Chasing who is *right*, or perhaps chasing validation within themselves as they try not to talk over one another
but always seem to end up doing anyway. The porch feels light, like
a cloud that Dante is imagining himself standing on. Grace's face
is every bit as beautiful as he remembers. A soft face unblemished
that once loved him and maybe parts of it still does. The sun beats
down on her skin, no warmth, only the afternoon summer sun that
looms over their lives. Her words are just the sound of baby birds
chirping. He is lost in the beauty of the woman he still very much
loves.

Mason screams from within the house. He cries for help, plead-
ing to see his mother who is unable to hear him. The sweat sneaks
down Dante's brow but feels like electricity dancing on the surface
of his skin while he stares into Grace's lips. Mason's screams grow
louder and the baby birds from Grace's mouth become her baby
boy's cries to leave with her. Dante tries to cover his ears but is
paralyzed, discovering only now that he is just a passenger in his
body, watching from the crowd as the scene plays out.

The cries become a ringing sound that pierces through his ears
courtesy of the headache that seems to trouble him. With the
sudden pulsating shot of pain, the warm sun falls away and Grace
stands frozen on the porch staring back at him. The porch light
comes on automatically in the absence of light only for the bulb to
burst and cast a deep darkness that feels like a damp unlit basement.

Grace's features shift seamlessly into a horrific parody of herself that contrasts the comfortable and complementary attributes that Dante has come to love. Her mouth hangs open like a fish out of water, desperate for air. Her eyes bulge from her face as the whites become bloodshot and tears run down her face. Her face becomes bruised as her head whips wildly and jerks in motion unnaturally, like she's being hit over and over. The jerky movements cease and she stares back at her ex-husband, lips now blue and mouth soaked in blood. Dante shivers watching, unable to turn away. Unable to blink, only flinch and squint.

He notices the marks on her neck and as he focuses, his hands suddenly fill the shapes to match his hands as he pulls her into the house. The ringing sound in his ears ensues until the front door is slammed shut and he awakes jolting upright in his bed, sweating and unable to catch his breath. Another nightmare.

Chapter Twenty-Seven

TUESDAY

Another morning of waking up to more missed calls, more text messages, and more social media notifications. People are concerned and some are asking questions. It's Tuesday, and today is the day that Dante is scheduled to meet with his therapist, normally in the morning, before heading off to church to start the week.

The morning unfolds like a new version of *normal*. Dante wakes up, goes to the bathroom, checks on Mason, who ignores him, and then makes breakfast. Today he toasts some frozen waffles and pours the last of the milk and takes it down to Mason where he is met with more silence. Medication and then meditation, and now it's almost noon and it's time to consider what to do with Karl's body downstairs. Sick to his stomach about what he's done, Dante can't stop reliving the moment from yesterday. He paces through the house, more fidgety today than before. He checks the windows with nervous eyes and paranoid body language that won't stop moving.

"I don't know what to do with the body, what do I do with the body?" he mutters to himself. "I didn't mean to kill 'em, Mason saw ... you saw, right?" he asks, staring at the ceiling, waiting for a response. "I know, I know, I know, I know murder is a sin, but," he stops with his eyes staring through the ceiling. "But what if I had no choice? I don't have evil in my heart. I am good. I'm an extension of your word, my Lord. I'm one of your sheep and you are my shepherd, you know my heart is pure, you know that I had the best intentions." Dante leans on the kitchen counter and hangs his head before running his hands through his hair. A tired wind leaves his mouth. "I'm trying to save my son. Your son sacrificed himself but that's not my boy. I need to save him! You know my intentions were good, you have to know, right!?" Dante stands up straight with cracks in his voice that struggle to hold back tears. Like a flood wall with cracks in the foundation. His voice softens. "I know the whole thing with intentions though ... the road to hell is paved with them ... I know I've been wrong to question you, God ... but hell is no place for me ... I'm still good ... I'm still ... yours ... right?"

Dante spaces out, deep in thought as he stands in his kitchen, lost on his feet. He no longer feels the watchful eye or the warm embrace of the God he grew up praising. His words spoken to the ceiling only moments ago suddenly feel hollow.

Empty.

Abandoned.

His concentration is shaken when the light sneaking in through the window over the sink breaks for a moment. Something, or *someone*, is on the side of the house. He leans over the sink and sees a man standing in the side yard between his and Barry's house. He studies the man tip-toeing to try and see into the house. The man stops and is walking toward Dante.

Dante jumps away from the window with his heart kicking and the panic of being found driving him to instinctively head for the back door. Mason's backpack that he uses for baseball is sitting against the wall beside the door and Dante grabs the insulated handle of a composite bat and slips it out from the side pouch as he opens the door and steps outside. The bottoms of his socks collect bits of gravel and loose mulch as he inches to the edge of the house to have a glance around the corner. He sees that it is Dr. Bryant.

The insidious pain creeps back as his headache returns. A sigh of frustration escapes his body as he watches his therapist, who apparently makes house calls. Unseen, Dante considers what to do, admiring the baseball bat. As he looks up, Dr. Bryant is walking toward him, and is stopped in his tracks when he sees Dante. "Shit!" he exclaims with surprise on his face. With his phone in hand, he takes slow steps toward Dante. "Dante, I called you back. The message you left me Sunday. It was very ... troubling."

Dante eyes the phone in Dr. Bryant's hand, completely unaware that he has even raised the bat readying himself to swing. The therapist sees Dante looking at his phone and he stares at it also. In that splinter of a second he takes his eyes off of his patient. The bat cuts through the air with a whooshing sound followed by a hollow pop sound that is so satisfying on the ball field, but shuddering to hear on the side yard. The impact sends vibrations through Dante's hands that make his palms tingle.

Dr. Bryant hits the grass like a bag of dirt. His phone falls free from his hand and Dante wastes no time smashing it with the bat. One violent overhead swing is followed by the next as the phone cracks and bounces off the grass.

Dante turns to the therapist with his chest rising and falling like an exaggerated breathing technique. Dr. Bryant is as still as steel as he lies on the grass. Dante picks up the phone and all of the loose pieces and sticks them in the trash can on the side of the house. He looks around the side of Barry's house to ensure there are no cameras or anything. You never know what precautions police officers take with their home security. No one in the neighborhood seems to have been walking by to notice what just happened.

Dante grabs his therapist's legs, pulling him through the grass and across the concrete patio that leads to the back door. He tosses the bat into the house, where it bangs against the floor louder than anticipated. He switches sides, from the legs to hooking his arms underneath the doctor's arms and around his chest to hoist his upper body off the ground enough to drag him inside. He sets Dr. Bryant down on the floor, winded as he pushes the door shut with his foot causing it to slam.

Chapter Twenty-Eight

Exhausted and in disbelief, Dante sits on the kitchen floor right beside his therapist. Chortling at how bad the situation is, he looks at the time. Nearly noon and a second body to figure out what to do with. *He isn't dead, thankfully,* Dante thinks, but now something will need to be figured out and a dead man in the basement with a child handcuffed and a doctor held captive is not going to bode well for anyone he tries to explain this to. At some point this man will wake up and difficult decisions will need to be made.

Rummaging through drawers, Dante finds duct tape and a pair of scissors. He drags a chair from the dinner table as he places it near Dr. Bryant. *The doctor's body is so much heavier than it looks when it's dead weight,* he thinks, as he hoists the man from the floor like a two-hundred pound bag of sand and leaves him in an imperfect seated position that will surely be uncomfortable to wake up in.

Holding his body upright, Dante finagles with the duct tape to get it loose and easy to use. Once he does, he begins wrapping it around the doctor's shoulders just enough to stabilize him to the back of the chair. Dante secures the man's legs to the chair's legs. He pulls his arms behind the chair and tapes them to the spindles as well as he can since his hands won't reach all the way around to be fastened together.

Dante stands and drops the roll onto the floor once he is done. He stares at the man bound to the chair. "What am I even doing?"

he asks himself. He carries over another chair and places it across from the doctor and has a seat. He studies the man he once confided in, certain that he would no longer be able to build on that routine progress and rapport they had before today. Dante observes patiently, leaned forward with his elbows resting on his knees, and his chin resting on his clasped hands. He waits for the man who knows some of Dante's greatest insecurities to come awake and offer a solution where everyone somehow wins. *Do therapists possess the ability to pull off miracles? Heart surgeons and other specialists do wonders all the time, why should this be any different?*

"Dad!" The silence breaks along with Dante's concentration as Mason shouts up from the basement.

Dante stands, looks at the clock to see it is already noon. He goes to the door, staring down. "Yeah, son?"

The handcuffs jingle against the pipe as he leans his head into the light to look up at his dad. "I'm hungry," he says in a whimpering voice that wrings out Dante's soul.

He looks back, over his shoulder, at the therapist duct taped to the chair as he hesitates. "Yeah son. I'll get you something."

The boy fades back into the shadows, out of sight, with more gentle clinging of the chains. Dante surveys the cabinets with the food becoming more scarce with each passing day and the festering need to get out of the house. He goes to the refrigerator to see very little in actual things to put together a meal, mostly condiments. The freezer drawer holds frozen meats that are no help right now since they will need to be thawed. More frozen sausage links, some corn dogs that have been freezer burned due to not being closed properly, and a bag of dino-shaped chicken nuggets live within the frosty chamber. He pours half of the bag onto a cookie sheet then pre-heats the oven and waits for it to beep. The chicken-filled breaded dinosaurs go into the oven and come out crispy and hot. Not long after, Dante throws them onto two plastic plates, one blue and clear, and the other an atomic green that Mason used more frequently when he was a few years younger.

Dante heads downstairs with two plates, a bottle of barbecue sauce and two bottles of water carefully under his curled fingers beneath the plates–a real balancing act. He sits one plate on the floor and slides it toward Mason as he extends a bottle of water only to be met with a suspicious stare. "Well go on ... take it," Dante offers.

Mason is slow to reach, wary of his father's actions, much like an abused animal when offered affection. He takes the bottle and the cold is a welcome relief against his skin. His eyes close in what seems to be the only comfort Mason has felt in days. Dante sits on the floor, with his back to the wall, just out of reach of Karl's body, but well within reach of the blood that has pooled on the floor and started to dry. The two sit in silence, eating slowly, dancing around the need to connect.

Dante snickers while spinning a poorly shaped processed T-Rex in his fingers. "You know, it wasn't too long ago when your mother and I would make dinner, and you never really wanted to eat what we ate." Dante stares across at his son, met with sad eyes. "You used to always ask for chicken nuggets instead. At least three, four nights a week." Dante shakes his head with a melancholy grin worn on his face. "You must think I'm a terrible father, don't 'cha?" Mason looks down at his plate, not engaging in the conversation, but letting his body language say what his mouth won't. "Yeah, I would think I was a monster too."

Mason reaches down for another nugget and as he holds it, he lets it stand on the plate as he looks up at his dad, the other arm wrenched back, outstretched thanks to the cuffs.

Dante looks away, running his hand through his hair, frustrated before standing up and pacing around. "You remember not too long ago, you and I," Dante laughs, "you and I used to sit at the dinner table, we would pretend these chicken nuggets were toys." Dante stops and lets his head rock back as he stares at the ceiling with a sigh. "You would roar at me while your little hand moved your food across the table and I would play right along with ya." The tears begin to well up enough to make his words retreat. Wind breaks through his lips in a hard exhale accompanied by a laugh. "You ... you would smile at me and make dinosaur noises and I would do it right back. You would laugh and laugh. Then you would roar again. You'd sneak a glance at your Mom ... her face." He leans against the wall, allowing the laughter to melt away and the tears to come through finally. "It was the cutest thing," he cries.

"You know that your dad loves you, right?" Dante asks with desperation hanging on his words. "I just ... I just," Dante gasps. "I'm in a difficult spot. I'm trying to, I'm trying to ..." he puts his index finger to his head. "Figure. This. Out." he says, jabbing the finger to his head aggressively to each syllable spoken. "Son, I can see you're scared. I know. I'm scared too. Daddy's scared too. If Daddy doesn't figure this out then you might never see me again ... I might never see *you* again, and that scares me. Do you understand? Please tell me you understand that."

Mason pushes the plate away, still with some chicken nuggets untouched, and he stands. "I think *Dad* needs help," he utters clearly. "I think maybe you should talk to someone," he grins as he locks eyes with Dante. "But that person isn't available to talk anymore, are they?" Mason's voice mimics the sound of a warped record melting as it plays. Dante stares on, terrified that this is happening again after feeling like they were making progress. "Your little talking friend left you didn't he? Just like God left you! Like your father! Like your wife! Just like everyone leaves you!"

He's right. Dante hasn't felt close to God in the way he needs to, not in a long time. His father passed away and Dante was in no way prepared for something like that, no one was. Grace couldn't take it anymore and when Dante was still reeling from the death of his father, she left him too. It only makes sense that his son—the person he loves most in this world—would be the logical progression in people in his life abandoning him.

Dante steps over Karl's body to avoid being within arm's length of Mason, who does nothing but watch Dante skedaddle up the steps.

Chapter Twenty-Nine

S everal hours have passed and the evening dusk is setting on the day. The missed calls have slowed a bit, but the notification numbers continue to climb each time Dante looks at his phone. Anxiety is cranked beyond max volume and at any moment the doctor in the kitchen is going to wake up–with an awful headache–and wonder where he is and why he's taped to a chair in his patient's house.

"Hey!" Mason shouts from the basement. "Dad!"

Dante goes to the top of the steps. Peering down, he offers no words, still suspicious of his son's possession and doubting if his son is even still in there. He looks and sounds like Mason, but only sometimes. Other times he sounds like something from an awful nightmare.

Mason leans his head into the light. "Can you bring me another water, please?"

Dante wants to ignore the demon but isn't prepared to let his son go just yet, so he drags his tired body to the fridge and takes one of the last few bottles from the inside of the door. Another descent into the basement, he hands his boy the cold bottle. "What about him?" Mason asks, pointing to Karl's still body on the floor with the water bottle.

"What about him?" Dante responds, confused.

Mason spins the lid off the bottle and drinks it with one long gulp. "Well if you're gonna bring me a refreshment, you should bring one for our guest, it's only right. You taught me that, silly." He tosses the empty bottle at his father's feet. "That's just being a good host now, isn't it?"

"What do you know about being a *good host*?" Dante asks with a tinge of attitude in his voice, just enough to match his face.

"I don't know about being a host, but your boy sure makes a *great* host," Mason's voice says, only now coming from Karl's body.

Perplexed, Dante's eyes dart from Karl to Mason as the two laugh in unison. "What is this? What do you even want with my boy?"

Laughter fills the room, much like the dingy mildew smell. "Holy man," Karl's voice says, from the body still on the ground with moving lips. "It isn't what we want with your boy, it's what we want from yooooou."

"Probably the same thing your wife wanted from you," Mason says.

"We just want you here with us. At home," Mason's voice says from Karl's mouth.

Mason jerks his shoulder aggressively, making the chains clink. "But you're too concerned with asking *God* for a way out!" the boy hisses, saying God's name in disgust.

"Hey, that's probably why she left you, huh?" Mason says from Karl's mouth.

The boy turns to look at his Karl puppet with a smirk unlike any face Mason would make on his own. "Such a sweet and wholesome woman...and this guy," he says, gesturing to Dante, still standing as a passive audience to the back and forth, "total nutcase."

The boy and the body on the floor turn their heads to face Dante. "I know what it is," Mason says.

"There's a reason she left you," they say in synch. They look at each other and back at Dante. "And it starts in the bedroom!"

The pair laugh and it reverberates against the walls. The demon has taunted Dante enough as he flees the basement with a bottled rage that doesn't match the paleness in his frightened face.

Chapter Thirty

D r. Bryant's head is rolling from shoulder to shoulder, stirring in restraint as Dante comes upstairs. The doctor's eyes creep open. The light causes him to tense up and his reaction is enough to make him aware of the knock on his head. "Ahhh," he lets out, acknowledging the pain.

"Try not to move," Dante advises.

"What–" the doctor stammers, face tight with confusion. "Dante?"

Dante has a seat across from his therapist. "I know you must have fifty questions right now, and I'm sorry about the tape, but I'm afraid I can't let you just leave."

Dr. Bryant stares down his patient with trepidation in his face. "Dante, whatever this is, whatever you're doing, you've gotta cut me loose. Something is happening and you've gotta let me help yo–"

"Something is happening, alright," Dante interjects with a smirk. "I don't know how much of that you heard down there."

Dr. Bryant stares at the open door to the basement, then back to Dante. "I'm ... I'm not sure what I heard," he says in a measured and even-tempered tone. "What do you think I heard, Dante?"

"Cut the act, doctor. I know your game here."

"There's no game, Dante. I'm taped to a damn chair in your kitchen. Who's playing games here?"

Dante stands up to lean against the kitchen counter. The gravity of the situation falling on his back. "Something is happening to my son, doctor," he says, ignoring him completely, "I don't know what to do."

Dr. Bryant watches Dante begin to pace, running hands through his hair. "What's going on with your son, Dante?" Dante continues to move back and forth in short distances through the kitchen. "Where is your son?"

Dante takes a seat, letting a long breath come out of him. "You've gotta help me. I need a solution."

Dr. Bryant sits with his jaw unhinged, "Listen. You're asking me for help, I came here to check on you because your phone call was clearly a cry for help ... you see that, right?" Dante stands again, sweat on his brow, face beet red. "I came here to *help you*, Dante. Let me help you."

"I do need your help. I might have really messed up. You have to believe me though when I tell you, okay?"

"What did you do? What happened?"

"It was Mason, he attacked me. He's been acting strange the last few days and one thing led to another and I kind of handcuffed him to the furnace."

"Kind of? What do you mean kind of? Where is he now?"

"He's downstairs."

"Mason!" Dr. Bryant calls out.

"Help me! Please! I need–" Mason's voice cries out as Dante storms over and slams the door, muffling the response.

"Look at me," Dante commands, getting in the therapist's face. "If we're going to come up with a solution, I need to trust you. You can't try anything funny."

"I'm here for *you*, what do you think I'm going to do?"

"You can't tell anyone. This ... this isn't what it looks like ... I know how it looks. I'm asking you to believe me."

"Dante, I don't want to do anything extreme here. You haven't done anything here yet that can't be undone or forgiven."

"I haven't told you everything yet."

"We can talk through it all and come up with a practical solution right now. But first, you have to cut me from this chair so I know I can trust you too."

"How do I know I can trust you?"

"Faith, Dante ... something you know a little bit about, yeah?"

"I'm not so sure nowadays."

"Okay ... how about doctor/patient confidentiality? You're still my patient as far as I'm concerned, I mean why else am I here?"

"You shouldn't have come here. I shouldn't have called you. I'm sorry."

"Don't apologize. You did call me, and now you need me more than ever before."

"No."

"And your son needs me now too, it sounds like." Dante shoots a glance at Dr. Bryant that could burn through him. "Look, you clearly recognize that there is trouble here. I can help you."

"What does help *look* like if I cut you loose?" Dante says with suspicion woven into his speech.

"I can get you help. We can call someone and have you taken to–"

"No!" Dante objects. "Not an option! This isn't about me! It's about Mason! Something wicked has a hold of my boy and I need to save him!"

"This isn't about Mason, can't you see? You're going mad!"

"Did you not hear me? My son ... has a demon inside of him."

Silence hangs between them as they stare one another down. "You have your child, who you love, who loves you, a prisoner in your basement, Dante ... let me get you help."

Dante crouches with unbridled energy raging through his body causing him to bounce in place. He buries his face into his knees. Dr. Bryant may be right, that realization creeps into Dante's thought process. Mason's face looking at him horrified streams in his mind like breaking news on the TV. The nightmare with Grace at the front of his thoughts like a stain on his heart. The sound of Karl's body tumbling down the stairs still echoes in his mind. The stench that seems to taint the air lately. "Maybe you're right."

"I'll make sure Mason gets back to his mother. You can still come back from this."

Dante stands, his head shaking 'no' as he walks over toward the stove.

"No!" the therapist pleads. "What are you doing? This isn't a good solution, Dante!"

"I don't know what else to do. I've tried talking to God ... I've tried talking to you."

"Hey, hey! Look ... look at me!" Dr. Bryant attempts to reason with Dante. Dante pulls open a drawer beside the stove and begins rummaging through utensils, tools, and other things that make a lot of noise when they move around. "Look at me! Don't do anything stupid!" Dr. Bryant starts to rock from side to side with the chair knocking against the floor. "Think about your son!"

Dante pulls out a long flathead screwdriver, the kind with the red and yellow jeweled plastic handle. He looks at it with uncertainty and grimaces.

"Think about the example you're leading for your boy. This sort of thing stays with a child and I know you don't want that for Mason."

Dante stands in front of him, knuckles white as his hand shakes, gripping the tool.

"What will your neighbors and friends think? They're gonna know eventually. What about your community?"

Dante's eyes stream, he morphs into a more fragile man. "What about them?" he asks. "What about me!?"

Dr. Bryant begins to cry, flinching at the closeness of Dante in his emotional state. "This isn't what God wants for you!" he shouts, in a desperate attempt to appeal to his profession.

Dante laughs in response. The chuckling carries for a moment. "Okay, okay ... so this isn't what God wants." Dante marches over to the basement door and rips it open, the wooden banging against the wall as he gestures to the stairs. "I guess this is what God wants for my son though, huh?"

The doctor melts down, tears bursting from his eyes, sobbing. "I don't know, just please let me go. I swear to God I won't say a word, I won't tell a soul, you'll never see me agai–"

Dante charges over to him. "You keep throwin' around the G word. Are you playin' with me too, doc? Or are you a demon too?" The fear strikes Dr. Bryant and his skin crawls with an unease he has never known in his own life, only seen and heard about from others. "You playing a game with me? Is this another game?"

"I don't know what you want me to do," he weeps. "I just want to help. I don't know where this is coming from. You have to listen to me and–"

Dante closes his eyes, and traps a deep breath in his chest as he impulsively backhand swings the head of the screwdriver into his therapist's chest. The breath is released and his face is just as surprised as Dr. Bryant's.

The doctor's breath seizes up, and Dante recognizes he has gone too far. He is in too deep and no amount of explanation can preserve his image as things have gone from bad to worse. It's not even a concern at this point, as acceptance has dug its trench in his mind. *The only way out is through,* at least that is what he tells himself. He jams the screwdriver in farther, feeling the resistance of the chest plate scraping the metal, vibrating through the handle, feeling the life drain out of his one time confidant. He forces it in, all the way to the handle and pushes so hard that the front legs of the chair lift off the floor and the chair falls back. Dr. Bryant slams back down and Dante rips the screwdriver from his chest.

He stands there holding it like a knife. Not quite the same, but the snapshot might as well be.

Dante is a murderer.

His adrenaline has him soaring and hyper-aware, but also hyper-reactive. Anxiety at its peak, and shock on his face, he throws the tool and it bounces across the dinner table and lands in the living room on the floor. The blood pumps out in furious gushes like when you drop an open gallon of milk on the floor and it glugs out for the first few seconds a little harder than the spurts that follow.

He stares at his chest. Dr. Bryant's eyes watching Dante. The betrayal is evident on his face as the blood escapes his heart.

Glug ... glug ... glug ...

"I could have," he struggles, choking on his own blood, "halp ... you." Blood spittle bursts from his lips through the choking.

He isn't dead yet. Dante knew in his heart that it would likely come to this and he didn't want to do it in a violent way. *I'm not a murderer,* he assures himself. The longer the man takes to die on his floor, the more panicked he becomes. The only guarantee in silence is to expedite his dispatch as a kind mercy. Dante sidesteps to the sink counter and rips the toaster from the wall. He kneels beside Dr. Bryant's head. "I'm so sorry," he whispers as he lifts his head gently and wraps the cord around his neck two times. He wrenches as hard as he can on it and closes his eyes trying to block out the sounds of life fading. The sounds of fighting. The sounds of suffering. Until only silence and stillness remain.

CHAPTER THIRTY-ONE

WEDNESDAY

The evening passes relatively quietly, all things considered. Mason spends parts of the evening crying for help and whimpering while Dante keeps the basement door shut and stays upstairs to avoid the sounds that break his heart. Before, Dante struggled to fall asleep, but now, he just doesn't sleep at all. He does chores around his bedroom and finds himself redoing them just to stay busy. Changing bed sheets, refolding clothes, reorganizing his closet, and dusting blinds in a tedious fashion. Unable to relax or sit still he goes into Mason's room. No sleep is the perfect time to clean up the broken glass from a few nights ago and also to put the clothes and drawers back in the dresser neatly after falling out. He makes his son's bed and continues pitter-pattering about the upstairs until the sun rises.

It's now Wednesday morning and more missed calls, but with slower frequency. Less new text messages and no new activity on YouTube, Facebook, or Instagram. Dante has had the entire night to mourn and sulk over the dispatching of his therapist, and Grace's new squeeze, Karl. In his mind he has accepted that he will at some point have to pay for his crime and he has wrapped his head around the fact that he is likely heading to prison. The challenge before that remains the same as it was the last four days.

What about Mason?

Evil has taken hold of his son and only he can cleanse the demon and save Mason. He will face the music and let the justice system do its thing, while enduring the whispers from his friends and neighbors once this story hits the front page of the local newspapers. The townsfolk who he has known for so long will turn on him just like they do anyone else over minor grievances. They will swoop down like the social buzzards they are and pick the bones of his reputation's corpse clean if it means they get to make small talk of it all to each other. It will no doubt spread like infection within the community. His fate is in God's hands, but he must ensure that his son is safe in the end. Dante is determined to save the soul of his boy, even at the cost of his own.

Later in the morning there is a knock on the front door. His initial reaction is to hide and hope no one sees him. Learning from the mistakes before, he does good not to be in view of the side window in the kitchen. Dante sits atop the steps to the upstairs where he is just out of view of the door. The tapping of something hard raps against the glass in the door.

Tap! Tap! Tap! Tap! Tap! "Mister Dante!" a stifled voice beckons, like a summoning of the pastor that inhabits this home.

Susan ... it was only a matter of time.

He watches her shadow move across the window, blurred by the thin white curtain that blocks the window.

Tap! Tap! Tap! A little louder this time.

Boom! Boom! Boom! Boom! she bangs, her fist knocking on the wooden part now.

"Dante! Are you in there?" she asks, her face pressed to the glass, her voice carrying behind the echo of the booming knock almost like she was inside the foyer already.

Dante bows his head. The headache sneaks into his temple and sends small pulses of pain through his head. A subtle tugging of pressure behind his eyes. Like a child trying to get his attention by tugging on his sweater. *If I don't answer, she might not go away. She might cause more attention by being loud ... or worse, she might start asking the neighbors questions.*

He runs a hand through his hair in a lame effort to fix it and pats himself down as if to undo any suspicious wear on his appearance. He resists the impulse to roll his eyes as he sees her silhouette through the glass. With a quick spot check of the doorway view, he confirms that the therapist should be out of sight, should she stick her nose into the house. Dante opens the door just enough to pop his head out and Susan stands there wearing a shocked expression on her face. "Hey Susan. What's going on?"

"Dante, have you not been getting my calls or my texts?"

"I saw," he answers and notices she immediately takes offense and doesn't try to hide it on her face. "I just haven't felt good."

"Well don't you think you should have told someone at least?"

"I am dealing with some other stuff right–"

"Where's Grace at?"

"Why does everybody keep asking for Grace?"

"Who is everybody?"

There it is, the nosy old lady, reaching for information like a professional. "What are you doing here Susan?"

She gasps. "I'm here to make sure you're alright for one. This is unlike you. Everyone is worried sick and asking about you."

"I'm fine. I'm just trying to handle some stuff and I'm dealing with an illness."

"Well, have you seen a doctor yet?"

Not the kind you mean. "I have. He asked that I rest. That's what I've been doing. I thought that you all could handle my absence for a few days."

Another gasp as she shakes her head, clearly disapproving. "You have to tell someone though. How do we know to take care of things if you don't talk to us, Dante?"

He scratches his scruffy five o'clock shadow with a clueless face. He knows she is right but there is no sense in pushing the issue. "Listen, you came by. I'm here. Everything is fine. I'll be back soon. I'll stop in, let's say ... Friday, yeah?"

"What time, Friday? My dog has a vet appointment."

Dante shakes his head and notices the pulsing and creeping pain of that familiar headache coming on. He winces in pain after acknowledging the presence of the ache and the sound of Susan's country bred voice suddenly feels like a high pitch piano playing badly as it sinks into water. Her voice and words submerge into that abyss and the blood pounding through his temple begs for him to just go to sleep. Her voice prattles on while he stands with his eyes closed, enduring. High pitched and muddy sound takes on a transformation in his ears. The sound is more in his mind as he focuses on the blinding sensation that puts tension on his brain and holds onto the back of his eyes like the reins of two strong horses stampeding ahead.

This isn't uncommon for her to talk to anyone who will listen. Dante is used to this, but right now is not the time. He has to get her to leave. The transformation of her voice is unlike anything he has heard before. It sounds like duct tape unraveling and being pulled over his ears. Over his mouth ... his nose ... until he can't breathe ... and right then his eyes open and the pain dissipates entirely.

Susan is gone and the two of them are no longer going back and forth on the front porch. Dante is sitting at his kitchen counter spaced out in the comfort of his self-imposed prison.

PART III

SAVING MASON

Chapter Thirty-Two

With the world coming to Dante's doorstep, he knows that it is only a matter of time before he is found out and exposed for his crimes. No amount of explaining or justifying his actions will be enough for him to feel heard, seen, or understood. The only thing left now is to fix this problem himself, by any means necessary. Banishing the demon was never going to be easy, but there are people out there, on the internet, who have cited successfully eradicating the evil.

With Susan sent away, Dante is back to stomping through the house with only his thoughts and the bodies in his home that need to be taken care of. The stench from the basement has somehow begun to smell worse upstairs.

They will have to wait though.

Mason needs to be saved and it needs to happen now. Right now.

Dante goes through the motions of preparing the items needed again for the at-home exorcism recipe. He blesses the water and makes it holy, only this time he finds the proper bottle rather than the bowl he attempted the first time. He retrieves his father's cross, and the family Bible before heading back to the computer for one more go at the list of instructions. He stops in the kitchen and in a precautionary act, grabs a chopping knife from the knife block on the counter. He tucks it carefully in his belt behind him.

He finishes browsing a lot of the same websites he already had before, many of them being bookmarked, and he has scribbled some notes in addition to his existing notes. His preparation is methodical and his focus is overshadowing the anxiety he had not too long ago, as his purpose has become clear to him. Time waits for no man and he can feel the walls closing in with each passing minute. He draws a long breath in and exhales even longer, "It's time."

As he descends into the dark prison built for pretend robbers and repurposed for possessed children, he holds the cross like a sword of divine light. The Bible rests under his arm with the holy water in his other hand—the Lord's weapons. He reaches the slate floor, steps around the now mostly dried pool of blood from Karl's body, and Mason stands to face his father. The cuffs drag across the pipe and whine against the metal.

"Let's try this again, shall we?" Dante asks, opening the Bible and going straight to the pre-selected prayers for the ceremony.

"What are you doing?" Mason mutters, fear wrangling his boyish voice.

Dante unscrews the small bottle with the other hand and holds his thumb over the mouth of the bottle, ignoring his son's words. "Please, God. I beg of you, release my boy of this ... parasite that has come from the darkest corners of Hell and taken him." He flicks his wrist and lets the water splash onto Mason.

Mason looks annoyed more than irritated by the spritzing as he turns his face away and twists his body to avoid being splashed. "Dad, stop it!" he shouts. "What are you doing?" he asks through held back tears.

"Our Father, Who art in heaven, hallowed be Thy name;" he starts. Mason continues to writhe and move away from the water. "Thy kingdom come; Thy will be done on earth as it is in heaven."

"Please!" Mason wails. "Stop it!" The words bring Dante to a pause as the boy's voice booms in his head like a strong wind and war trumpets.

"Give us this day our daily bread," he continues. "And forgive us our trespasses as we forgive those who trespass against us; and lead us not into temptation, but deliver us from evil. Hail Mary, full of grace." Dante draws back the water and closes the Bible. He sets it on the workbench and holds the cross out, away from his body and pointed at his son. "Demon! There's no use in hiding anymore. You are before God, and Jesus Christ. And we command you to show yourself!"

Mason cowers as much as his chain will allow him to. He cries loud with deep sobs as the terror grips him in a way that makes Dante feel like the worst father ever. "I cannot let this deter my work. This is just another one of the devil's tricks and I will not falter."

Mason's voice, childish and small, attaches to Dante's mind. He no longer hears the world happening around him, only the memories of his little boy just being an innocent kid. The screaming and begging replace those memories though, as Dante focuses on what he knows needs to be done.

Dante rushes his son and grabs him by his tank top and presses him to the wall. Mason's face shatters into an ocean of tears, pale face, and quivering lip. Dante's heart breaks looking into his son's blue eyes as he recognizes the color in them, and the humanity in them for the first time in days. *I mustn't break. Not now,* he assures himself, committing to the exorcism, no matter how extreme. With his arm pinning the small boy to the concrete wall behind him, he reaches back and draws the knife from his belt and puts it to Mason's neck.

"Dad! Stop! Please!" Mason begs. "I love you! Please, please, please, I'll be good! I don't want to die! Let me go!" he squeals. "Let me go!"

"Stop begging! Show yourself, demon!" Dante orders, pressing the blade against his throat just a little more, and pinning him to the wall just a little harder.

Suddenly a bright white light floods the basement from atop the stairs and a voice follows.

Chapter Thirty-Three

Moments before.

The sound of a Honda motor hums as it shakes the frame of Barry's custom bike from his garage. The afternoon is gorgeous, perfect for leaving the doors and windows open. Tinkering isn't uncommon for Barry, whether it's his truck, his motorcycle, or piddling around the yard with anything that keeps his hands busy. The intoxicating drums of "Panama" by Van Halen pound from the speaker of a small boombox along with the wailing of David Lee Roth as he sings along, imitating the guitar riffs where he doesn't know the lyrics.

The door inside the garage that leads into the house creaks open and his wife, Barb, comes out. She turns down the radio and stands beside her husband, placing a gentle hand on his back and rubbing as he stands. "Hey mama," he says as he kisses her on the cheek.

"You almost done, hun?"

He pulls off his glasses, wiping the perspiration from his face with the front of his shirt. "Yeah, I think I'm about done for now." He kills the motor and stuffs the key in his pocket.

"Do you think you can use your big strong muscles and bring those bags of gravel to the backyard in a bit?" she asks, her voice soft and sweet with doe eyes to compliment. "I'd like to start on those flower beds."

"I'll get ya here in a minute, baby." He takes a sip from a big thermos, the ice bangs around and he sighs, refreshed.

Barb wraps her arms around him and the two sway in the garage as the sunshine pours in. "You're all sweaty," she says, with a coy smile, standing on her tiptoes to kiss him. "I made some macaroni salad, why don't you come eat first?"

He puts his glasses back on, "I should probably get that gravel for you before I get too comfortable. I'll be there in a few."

"Alright," she says as she heads back in. She stops at the door, "I'll get you some tea."

"Thanks, baby."

Barry strolls over to his truck and eyeballs the four bags of heavy pea gravel. He stands there for a moment, looking around the quiet neighborhood and he realizes there are a lot of cars on the street this afternoon. Some are familiar, and others less. The yellow Jeep parked behind Dante's car in the driveway has been there for days, which is odd for Dante, who doesn't often have many visitors. Three other cars are on the street, one blocking the driveway, the others in front of the house.

A nagging intuition is clawing at his gut as he passively tosses a bag of pea gravel over his shoulder and begins to make the journey to his backyard. As he walks through the grass along his side yard, he can't help but to notice the windows of Dante's place. The curtains pulled shut in a way that he isn't used to seeing. Barry never made a habit of peeping through windows or anything but has always been vigilant enough to notice he could see into the house at minimum. Something seems off, in a way that has his cop brain screaming to further investigate.

He plops the bag onto the already prepared flowerbed and he walks over to Dante's yard. He notices that the grass is a bit taller than normal and finds it alarming that Dante hasn't been as active in lawn care. Dante is pretty routine about cutting his grass on Wednesday and Saturday mornings and there hasn't been any rain so something is definitely up.

When did I see him last? Saturday? Sunday? Yeah, it was early Sunday. Connecting the dots of what seemed like—at the time—nothing worthy of suspicion. Pastors and church folks get up early on Sundays. The added element of Dante being kind of rough though and his comment about not sleeping well has Barry's gears turning. He opens the trash can and sees a few bags of trash but notices the shattered cell phone on top. *Well, that's a red flag. Maybe it was Mason's. Why is it smashed so badly?*

Barry peeks through the kitchen window and there is only a small opening to see inside. He sees the curvature of the tall sink faucet and that's when Barry's suspicions are confirmed. His eyes light up and he nearly stumbles backwards at the sight of two shoes pointing to the ceiling attached to a pair of legs taped to a chair. That's all he can see from there but the police training and instincts kick in and he is racing back to his garage. He grabs his phone and dials as he walks into the house. He moves right past Barb, walking with a purpose.

She knows something is wrong. "What's the matter, honey?"

"Something is going on next door," he says as he walks into their bedroom and pulls a gun from his nightstand and a flashlight from the footlocker on the floor in their closet.

"What's going on? You're scaring me."

"Stay in the house, mama."

A dispatcher answers the phone. "9-1-1 what is your emergency?"

"Yeah, this is Officer Barry Hale, I need backup, send officers to 225 Fairview Drive. Domestic issue, possible injuries, possible casualties. Send immediately."

Barry looks at his wife as he chambers a round in his police issued service weapon. "I'm serious, baby, don't leave the house. I'll be back." He leans forward and kisses her. "I love you." He rushes out of the house and back over to Dante's as he climbs the stairs to the porch and surveys the scene. Even though the curtains over the window are see-through it is still too difficult to see much of anything clearly.

Barry hangs around the porch waiting for backup to arrive as he works on his day off. He has another look into the window to try to see through and he hears the screaming. Screams that he is all too familiar with in his line of work. Barry front kicks the door, placing his Skecher just under the door knob and splintering the door frame on impact as the door whips open and bangs off the wall inside from the explosive contact. With his pistol raised, he steps inside and the screaming is clear. Barry's stomach tightens and twists at the sound of a young boy begging and screaming.

Upon entry, he sees a woman's body on the floor, poorly hidden behind the couch, face disfigured, pale, and bloodied. Grace Mitchell, friend and former neighbor. Another man taped to a chair in the kitchen, not moving. And another female on the floor behind the other sofa, motionless as well. No time to attend them given the screaming but the ambulance and backup would surely be on it when they arrive and see the bodies.

Barry takes careful steps through the house as he follows the shrieking and sees the basement door open and the echoes from the screaming threaten to haunt his nightmares for the rest of his life. He turns on the flashlight, shining it into the basement, horrified by what he sees.

CHAPTER THIRTY-FOUR

"Freeze!" Barry orders, taking a few steps into the basement with his weapon drawn. "Dante, put the knife down and step away from the boy."

Dante pivots behind Mason quickly, retreating from the bright light as Barry takes another step down. "Go away Barry. This doesn't concern you. This is between God and us."

Barry aims the light and notices the handcuffs that he gave Mason, holding him prisoner. That sickening feeling overwhelms him. To know that he gave those to a young boy in a gesture of playfulness and imagination wreaks havoc on his conscience. "What the fuck did you do, Dante?"

Mason's eyes stare into Barry's soul, shiny from the tears and shaken from the fear. The whimpers, the sobs, all too much not to distract the friendly neighbor. Doing the job everyday for so many years is one thing. He is able to compartmentalize to a degree, but this is different. He's known Mason since before he could walk. "Mason, look at me," Barry says, taking another careful step down. Mason's lip quivers from his shaking jaw as he listens to the man with the gun. "Are you okay?" Barry then notices the wound on his thigh and the blood that has run down it.

Barry isn't oblivious to the body on the floor with the pool of dry blood either. His training has taught him to preserve the living and how to handle these situations. Mason doesn't say anything, he just continues to sob, frightened in his father's grasp with the knife to his neck.

"Barry, I asked you to leave. Don't take another step. I'm telling you!" Dante threatens.

"Dante, just put the knife down. I'll put the gun down. We can talk ... we're neighbors. Friends ... let me help you."

"Why does everyone want to talk!?" Dante expels through ragged breath. "I told you to leave!"

"You know I can't do that, I can't just walk away with Mason in danger."

"No, no, no! Don't you understand? *I'm* the one that's in danger, not him!" Dante hisses. "He's been terrorizing me for four days. The exorcism didn't work. God never came! He doesn't care! He–"

"Listen to me," Barry says, with an even-tempered, yet affirming voice. "Step away from the child ... don't make this any more difficult for me, please," Barry nearly begs, hoping things don't escalate.

"I just wanted to save my son," Dante begins to cry. His body loosens and his head hangs.

"You can't hold your son captive like this."

Dante raises his arm, pointing the knife at Barry. "*You* didn't see what was happening here! *You* don't have a clue!" he says, gritting his teeth. "I can't be locked up while this demon has my boy."

"What was your plan here?"

"I thought I would be able to scare off the demon, in the name of Jesus. I didn't think it would come to this."

"This is child abuse. Kidnapping." Barry takes another step down, his eyes fall on Karl's body. "Murder!" Barry reaches the basement floor and looks back at Dante. "What did you think was gonna happen?"

"I thought I would save my son."

"There are three people upstairs, dead. This guy. Dead. And you thought–"

"Whoa, whoa," Dante cuts in. "Three people?"

Barry keeps his weapon raised, focusing on Dante. Mason's arm is raised thanks to Barry's cuffs and Dante is securely standing behind, crouched, too close to risk firing a weapon.

"I saw the bodies coming in. What did you expect when a policeman walks into the house and there are two bodies behind couches, a man fastened to a chair, and a man holding a knife to his injured and frightened child?"

Dante stares at the floor, then to Karl, and back at Barry, his eyes behind a palisade of tears and words imprisoned in his throat. "What about *me* being frightened!?"

"Just put the knife down. Don't do anything stupid!" Barry orders. "You can still come out of this without anyone else getting hurt."

Dante's lips tighten and his eyes wince. The tears fall and repel down his face. "Karl, he was an accident. I didn't mean to. And Dr. Bryant, I ... I had to make ... I couldn't let him stop me from saving my boy."

"You killed the mother of your child. Do you realize how this looks?"

"I didn't! She left! I watched her leave! That was Sunday!"

"She's upstairs on the floor behind your damn couch!"

Puzzled and heartbroken, he tightens his arm around Mason, who whines against the added pressure. "I made her leave though. She can't be *dead*."

Barry realizes just how unhinged his neighbor is now. This isn't a matter of a sick killer in a standoff. This is the matter of a sick man in need of help who didn't get it. "There's a whole parking lot of cars outside your house. How do you think I thought to check on ya in the first place?"

Dante's world crashes through the reality he has known for the last four days. It could be even longer. His thoughts scramble and his words come out muted. Heavy boots dance across the wooden floors upstairs and he looks up at Barry with a wall of light shining down around him from atop the steps. Silhouettes of more men fill the doorway as the blinding light rains in.

With his arm around Mason's neck he feels the blood raging, warm and pulsating against his skin. Dante loosens his chokehold enough to allow Mason to move away as the clarity washes over Dante. Mason shuffles to the wall in a hurry. The handcuffs drag across the pipe as he hugs the wall with his back against it.

The world feels darker and a little more empty.

Dante's future, a little more certain—even if not for the better.

He raises his hands to surrender, letting the knife fall to the floor. The world slows like the moment is sedated. The obsessive thoughts of what others might think melt away and the guilt rips through his shoulder in the form of a gunshot as the muzzle flare lights up the room.

The sound is muted.

Dante hits the cold floor. The smell of damp, moldy basement clouds his thoughts, crippling him. Everything goes black and the pain doesn't come. He sees Mason's face, smiling and laughing. He's young and innocent again.

No trauma from being held prisoner by his father.

No heartache from witnessing Mommy and Daddy fight.

Not a care in the world.

Dante smiles at the thought.

Hands grab Dante's body and he is weightless. His arms are twisted and contorted as he is restrained before floating away on a cloud. Vivid feelings that are much more rough upon waking up. Policemen in bulletproof vests carry him up the steps as his hands are zip tied behind his back. His eyelids are heavy and the voices aggressive. His knees and shins bang off of every step as he is dragged up. His shoulder is warm and wet as it pulsates and thumps to the rhythm of his heart. He fights to open his eyes with hopes to see and talk to his son.

As he is carried across the kitchen, he sees his doctor there, duct taped to the chair. Things didn't have to end this way. In the living room, the couches are pulled away from the walls and in the center of the room. He sees the first body. An older woman, a head of short white hair hangs over a face completely wrapped in duct tape. Dante's head begins to ache at the realization that Susan is dead on his kitchen floor.

Through the living room the headache is only worse as he sees Grace, the love of his life, lying on the floor, face and neck bruised and bloodied. Her skin, as pale as an overcast cloud that hovers over his life. It is only a passing glimpse but the disbelief crumbles at the sight of her. Dante gives up the fight to stay awake and his head lulls as he is carried out of the house and everything goes black.

Chapter Thirty-Five

His body is heavy as he tries to move. Lifting his leg is such an intensive task that he gives up quickly. The effort is exhausting as he comes to. Eyes prying open, begging to close as the fluorescent light pours in. His head rocks to the side to ward off the brightness. His hand raises to cover his eyes and is met with resistance.

Klink.

Handcuffs slide against the metal rails of a hospital bed.

Dante's hand drops to his side and he raises his head preparing to scoot himself into a more seated position when he is slowed by the light-headedness of moving. He slumps back down and his eyes adjust to the room, taking in his surroundings. A machine hums beside his bed where a cord runs up to his finger monitoring his heart rate. He notices the IV also plugged right into his arm with a dripping pouch connected. His shoulder is bandaged up and the Yankees are playing the Blue Jays on the small TV mounted on the wall with the volume turned down.

The door opens and a young woman in powder-blue scrubs walks in. "Oh, hey," she says with wide eyes and infectious enthusiasm. "You're awake!"

Dante groans in response as his face follows her across the room. "Where ... where am I?"

"You're at the Mercy Hospital in Anderson," she answers, fidgeting with a machine and writing something on her notepad. "And my name is Bethany and I'll be your nurse until about eleven o'clock tonight."

Dante's head feels weightless and heavy all at once, like he doesn't have control of his movements. "Why am I handcuffed?"

Bethany doesn't answer him right away, she finishes her scribbling. "I will go get your doctor and let him explain it to you. Are you feeling hungry or thirsty? Need me to get you anything?"

Dante closes his eyes. "No, I don't think so."

"Okay then, hang tight. I will be right back with the doctor."

Bethany leaves the room and is gone for less than five minutes, but for Dante, it feels like twenty-five. *I should be in pain,* he thinks. *They must have me drugged up.* The door opens and Bethany comes back in with a man dressed more like an accountant than the traditional white coat doctor.

"Good evening Mr. Mitchell, my name is Doctor Clark. How are you doing?" he asks, pulling a stool over to Dante's bedside.

Dante is slow to move. "I feel like a bag of dirt, thanks for asking."

"Yeah, it figures you might. We've got you on meds for the pain right now so that makes sense."

"Hey doctor."

"Yes?"

Dante tugs on the cuffs. "Why am I cuffed to the bed?"

Dr. Clark pauses for a moment and shoots a glance to Bethany who stops what she is doing and leaves the room. As the door closes behind her, he lets out a weighted breath. "Okay. I just want to be transparent before we get into it. There is a uniformed police officer outside your room. You're currently in police custody, I'm sure he will be in shortly."

Dante turns his head away toward the window, staring at the light that glows through the closed blinds.

"What can you tell me about the last week or so?"

Dante turns back slowly, staring at the TV. Aaron Judge's massive frame, draped in Yankee pinstripes hulks over home plate. "I remember ..." He pauses as the recollection is fuzzy and escapes him. Aaron Judge takes a swing at the first pitch for a strike. "I remember Mason, he was acting scary ... I was scared."

The doctor turns to see what Dante's eyes are fixated on, as Judge hits one to deep right field for an out. "What was Mason doing that you were afraid of?"

"You won't believe me."

"Try me."

"Do you believe in God, doctor?"

Dr. Clark stares at Dante, tapping the pen against his leg, considering carefully. "I believe in God, yes."

"So you believe in the devil then?"

"I suppose I do then, yes."

"I believe my son was possessed."

"I see," Dr. Clark says. "Can you tell me how he came to be handcuffed to the HVAC unit in your basement?"

Dante's face becomes neutral, void of expression. "I remember him being down there. I remember my father and his mother speaking to me through him."

"What can you tell me about the others that were in the house?"

Dante takes his eyes away from the TV and turns away, letting his silence speak for him.

The doctor stands with a grunt to break the silence. "Well I'm gonna leave you be for a bit. I will be back later. The nurse will be in to take care of you through the evening. If you need anything from me, let her know and I will be right in."

He goes to the door and as his hand grips the handle Dante turns his head. "Is my son ... is he okay?"

Dr. Clark stares back at him for a moment. "Your son is fine. He is being treated for his injuries and will be taken care of," he says with an even-tempered and professional delivery.

He turns the handle and leaves, letting the door ease shut and the click from the door shutting is the last thing Dante hears before he cries himself to sleep in the hospital, held to the bed by a pair of cuffs.

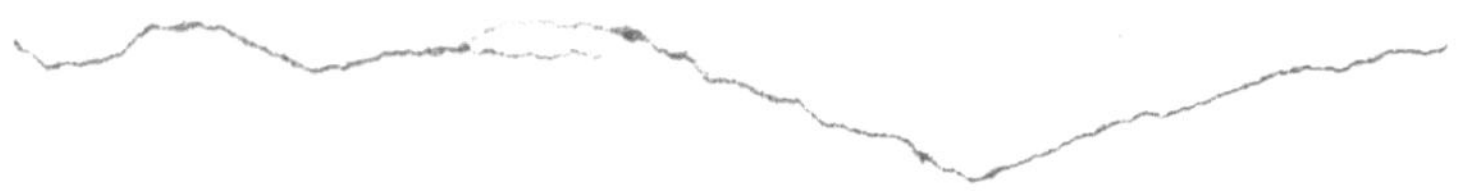

Dr. Clark is sitting in a cramped office just down the hallway, where he is providing a detailed rundown of Dante Mitchell and his current status to another doctor.

The other doctor leans against a desk with a folder in his hand, open as he reviews documents. His concentration makes his face tighten. "I would say, based on the evidence and everything in Mr. Mitchell's file, that he is suffering from some undiagnosed comorbidities. You've read the file. What do you think?"

Dr. Clark leans back in his chair as the back of it cries against his weight. "I would have to agree with you. You're the expert in this matter though. How do you want to move forward with treatment?"

The other doctor stands upright, pacing the short distance between desks in the narrow office space as he continues reviewing the paperwork. "Hmm," he begins. "If I were to take a stab at it, I want to say based on what we know after speaking with the police officer, who is the neighbor, and after reviewing his files from his therapist," he closes the folder and crosses his arms with a finger tapping just below his lip. "I'm going to suggest that our patient is—and possibly has been—dealing with delusional disorder, with episodes of derealization, possibly from stress, maybe an amalgamation of many events or changes that led to this."

"Is that a suggestion or a diagnosis, doctor?"

The doctor grunts with a smirk. "It's a diagnosis. We can determine based on a previous diagnosis from his therapist that I was able to dig up, but there is clearly more going on with the patient." The doctor sits the folder on a desk and pulls out a form and scribbles his name across the bottom before handing it over to Dr. Clark. "We will need to have him sent to a psychiatric center to be monitored for now. Begin a regime of meds and let's get him to a good headspace where he can talk with us. I'm sure the police and investigators will be eager to chat with him as well."

The doctor slides the folder across the desk to Dr. Clark, who reviews the orders and moves forward as instructed.

Chapter Thirty-Six

Mason is treated for his injuries and his grandparents come to be with him in the hospital along with other relatives. He stays overnight to be monitored as he is shaken up pretty badly. He meets his social worker for the first time, Mary Adams. Part of Mason being dismissed comes with a lot of red tape and some of that involves the cooperation and witness statement of what happened in that house.

The severity of the situation means that the best recount has to come within a short time of the events taking place, but there is sensitivity considering it is with a child who went through hell.

After initially meeting and the grandparents having their hands held through this delicate and at times frustrating process, Mason is ushered into a room where he meets with Mary privately while his family waits outside.

Mary invites Mason to have a seat on a sofa across from where she sits in an decorative upholstered chair with only an open space between them. The room is calming and quiet as Mason sits upright like he is rebelling against the comfort of leaning back. Mary studies the boy's physical behavior and notices his busy hand movements and how curious his eyes are as they scan the room. He sits in his hospital gown and she can see part of the bandage from where his leg was treated.

"Tell me, Mason," she begins, shattering the awkward silence hanging in the air. "What's your favorite subject in school?"

Mason's eyes land on her, but his words stay with him.

Mary does well not to pry for too much too quickly. Her questions need to be intentional and appropriate in a way that she has to think like a ten year old.

"How about video games, do you like video games?"

He nods his head yes.

"Okay, well," she leans forward. "I like video games too." Her eyes open, revealing a pair of comforting blue eyes and a disarming smile to match them. "What games do ya like to play?"

Mason shrugs, his eyes meeting hers. "Minecraft," he says softly.

"Dude," she says, very spirited, spreading her hands with a surprised face. "I love Minecraft!"

"You do?" Mason asks, suspicious of her enthusiasm.

"Uh, yeah ... my little brother plays it all the time. I've played with him a few times. He's about your age. His name is Caleb."

The two discuss video games in vague detail as Mary tries to loosen him up. His walls are up but she has done this long enough to know these things often take time and she just needs to focus on being a strong support system for him and keep his best interest. Mason's body language suggests that he is not comfortable still but he isn't unwilling to talk either.

"Mason, I need to ask you some questions," she begins, maintaining her soft and inviting tone. "About your dad, and the last few days." Mason tenses up, shuffling his butt within the seat. "Would that be alright?"

Mason nods, uncertainty heavy on his face.

"Can you tell me," she pauses as she considers how to ask this child the tough questions. "How did you end up in the basement?"

The quiet is heavy as he stares at the floor for a moment. "My dad was yelling. He woke me up."

"Why did he wake you up?"

"He was saying that I had something bad inside of me and he needed to figure out how to help me."

"Do you remember how long you were down there?"

Mason shakes his head *no*.

"Ok. Can you tell me about the first time he hurt you?"

"He was saying things and kept hugging me. He looked scared."

"What was he scared of? Did he say?"

"Me."

"I bet that scared you too, huh?"

Mason nods his head.

"Can you tell me about the bruises?"

"He dragged me out of my bed. I hit the dresser when I was trying to pull away from him. I tried to hide in the corner and my dad started crying and throwing things. He was yelling a lot. He broke the light in my room too."

"Did he," Mary hesitates to ask as she doesn't want him to lose his nerve. "Touch you? Inappropriately?"

"He kept grabbing my arm and squeezing me really tight. It hurt." Mason bends his elbow with a grimacing expression. "He hurt my elbow pretty bad."

Mary's face contorts where she fights her sad expression. "Has your dad ever acted like this before?"

Mason shakes his head *no*.

"So what happened after that?"

"He dragged me downstairs."

"And that's when he handcuffed you?"

"Mhm. He was throwing more stuff. Tools and anything that was out."

"All while you were cuffed to the furnace, huh?"

"Mhm."

Mary adjusts in her seat, considering how to move this conversation forward without it being *too much* for the child. Her gaze keeps being pulled to the visible bandage on his leg. "Can you tell me about your leg?"

He turns his body and pulls on his hospital gown in an attempt to hide the bandage as his eyes move back to the floor. "That's where he stabbed me."

"He stabbed you? With what?"

"A fork."

"And he had you sleep in the basement like that?"

"Yeah."

"Did you eat? What about if you had to potty?"

"I was eating ... he gave me a bucket to use."

"You used the bathroom in a bucket?" she asks with shock in her eyes.

"Yeah."

"So you slept down there. What did your dad do while you were downstairs that whole time?"

"He would come downstairs to bring me food, sometimes to ask me weird questions."

"What kinds of questions?"

Mason shrugs. " I don't really know." Mary begins to write things down. "He kept calling me a demon."

"And this must have confused you quite a bit."

"He seemed really scared of me."

The room falls silent and the emptiness screams. "What can you tell me about some of the things you might have been able to hear upstairs?"

Mason shifts in his seat. "I heard arguing and screaming."

"Other people?"

"Yeah. My dad was angry."

"Do you know what about?"

"Not really. But I heard fighting."

"Did you recognize any of the people?"

"My mom was the first one to come by, but I didn't know what happened at first. And then Karl." His eyes start to water after the mention of his mother.

"And Karl was your mom's new boyfriend?"

"Yeah. I saw my dad hit him and come downstairs and kill him."

Mary feels her eyes welling up and wipes them, taking a moment to collect herself. "So the policeman that came into the house, he was your neighbor?"

"Mister Barry, yeah."

"He shot your dad when he had a knife to you. Do you know why your dad had the knife to you?"

"No. He just kept telling me he needed to get it out of me and he was mad at God ... that's when Barry came."

"And that's when he saved you and you learned about your mom."

Mason sits staring at the floor as the grief washes over him.

"I think it would be okay to leave this alone today." Mary stands up, giving a nod to grandma who is waiting outside, staring through a tiny window in the door. Mary goes over to Mason, and kneels beside him and lifts his chin. His grandparents enter the room and the three grownups surround Mason. "You've been very helpful and very brave by sharing with me Mason, and I know how hard it must be. I want you to know that I am here for you and if you need anything at all, let your grandparents know and they will make sure to tell me so I can get you what you need."

Grandpa rubs Mason's back as he leans into his grandma. Mary stands and lets the family have their privacy as she makes her exit. The boy and his family grieve in the loss of his mother, their daughter, and the idea of Mason having a place to sleep, and a family to take him in despite the fleeting feeling of safety and security. The trauma paves a road that should only be traveled in a vehicle of healing and therapy. The inescapable feeling of being alone despite the love around him brings on a darkness within that covers him like a warm blanket.

"I know this is hard now, but we're here for you sweetheart. Don't you worry honey," Grandma reassures him, sobbing into Mason's shoulder.

Mason leans his head into the crook of her neck and closes his eyes. The tears form at the memory of being at home with mom and dad when everyone was happy.

No one was angry.

No one was yelling.

No one was dead.

Epilogue

The community of New Richmond is rattled after the events that took place in their small little river town. The home of their beloved and respected pastor became a homing signal for anyone with a badge for several weeks following the events that took place. Investigators and journalists seemed to flock to anyone who knew Dante or had any ties to the church. The town being so small and tight-knit, it seemed like everyone knew him in some way at one point in time.

As Dante's home was eventually foreclosed, so was the property of the church. With it being a small independant church, many of the members who worked closely with Dante were not able to put up money for the church–in addition to also having no interest in running it–but they were sensible enough to seek opportunities for a collaborative partnership with a parent church that has a network of churches throughout the city. Within that network there were plenty of pastors chomping at the bit to come speak the gospel to a devoted group. Everyone seems to be taking to this transition well.

A memorial service was held at the church a week after the passing of Susan, Grace, Karl, and Dr. Bryant. Folks came from all over the tri-state area to pay respects along with sympathetic parties following the story of this horrific event. It was a celebration of life where people were sad, some visibly destroyed, and others sought opportunities to uplift others. That night a candlelight vigil was held outside of the church where somber folks gathered to say their farewells and also console the survived families.

Barry Hale went on to be recognized as a community hero and to be held at the highest esteem in the public lens. The friendly neighbor and soon-to-retire police officer's face could be seen across all major news networks for up to a week after the murders at the Mitchell house. The initial interviews were just Barry sticking to the facts and mostly him declining to comment on Dante himself or his relationship as a long time neighbor. Since things have calmed down and everyone has gone on about their lives, Barry still gets the occasional call from some news outlet wanting a detailed article or a true crime podcaster wanting to sink their teeth into his brain and suck out the gory details. He continues to decline with no intentions of disclosing more than the police report shows. He has turned down a possible book deal that would see him writing a tell-all tale of his afternoon heroics.

Barry and his wife Barb have plans to enjoy his retirement and police pension, spending their days spoiling their grandchildren in hopes they never have to experience a side of human nature that Mason had to experience.

Mason's maternal grandparents took him in without hesitation once the social worker made sure it was a safe environment for him. Mason's injuries were minimal aside from the leg wound and the dislocated elbow that somehow popped back into place, but is still causing him some grief. He experienced lots of bruising in those days and he has taken to living with his grandparents as well as you could hope for. The social worker does a great job to meet with him and coordinate his visits with the parade of doctors and specialists that are involved in his ongoing treatment. The trauma he underwent has paved a long road ahead.

The social worker and grandparents communicate well and all decisions are made in the best interest of Mason. They have agreed to meet at a private office for most visits due to Mason's anxiety anytime someone knocks on the door or the doorbell rings. It's easier for them to just take him out of the house to ease him into a comfortable and safe space. Mason is okay for the most part. As okay as a child can be after that horrific experience. Watching his father come undone and hearing everything he heard, and seeing the things he'd seen will have lasting effects, but with caring and loving adults in his life looking out for him he will be equipped with the tools to manage.

The guest room in the grandparents' home becomes his bedroom. He sleeps with the door open and a light on always, something that is new in his life. His grandmother is spearheading his homeschool routine in the meantime, just until he is ready to go back to school. He expresses how he misses his friends and he enjoys seeing some of them at church on Sundays. That small opportunity to see friends is the only thing that distracts him at church and helps him not to think about his dad. He has always associated church with his dad and grandfather, so it is nice to not constantly think about it.

Most nights, he wonders where his dad is and how he's doing. He hears whispers sometimes about his dad being in a hospital and other times hears of prison and a court sentence, but he doesn't understand what it all means.

Every night, and every morning he thinks of his mother. He misses her and when he thinks about her he hates his dad for what he did. Many nights he has cried, and many nights he has had nightmares that keep him up through the morning. This is a big contributor to the decision to homeschool. Grace's name is mentioned often and she is so loved and even more missed. Grandma and Grandpa have a house decorated with family photos and Grace's face is all throughout the house at various stages of her life. Seeing photos of her smiling makes him smile and after months of living with them, he has begun to grow closer with his grandmother and even ask questions about what she was like when she was younger. She tells him that his mom grew up in the same house and that helps him somehow feel a little closer to her.

On the wall Mason notices a familiar photo of him with his parents. One that used to hang in his home when he lived with both of them. It stayed at the house after he and his mother left and it never moved. The photo shows the three of them smiling, not yelling or fighting. The photo makes him sad, but also, it brings a sense of peace that lets him remember the times when they all had a reason to smile.

Acknowledgements

This story is one that I have had rattling around in my head since 2019. When my friend and I began messing around with the idea of making micro films for Youtube it had set a fire in me creatively. I was eager to learn more about operating the Canon 80D camera and the various lenses while also writing screenplays with intent to film ourselves. My buddy Todd Condit also was throwing gas on this fire of mine by sharing some things he had done with minimal resources and I want to say it was after we completed our first (and only) project that I started writing a ton of things.

I had an idea that I couldn't quite figure out how to execute but I loved the idea of and ultimately that was the seed for what this book is. I imagined it being more of a found-footage style horror film told through the lens of a laptop webcam. I never wrote the screenplay so we couldn't film it as I originally envisioned it but I am happy that this story was so unforgettable to me because over the years I continued to shape and layer different elements to the characters and things I wanted to talk about through this story.

I'd like to give a big shout out to Shantel Brunson, author and (I think) the only snake person I know (She has snakes, she isn't like some snake/human hybrid though. Those don't exist in real life). In 2022 I reached out to a group chat full of authors asking for insight about mental health diagnosis sources and how to determine that, along with medications etc. Shantel's assistance with those things opened the road for me to begin outlining this story and really building what it would become. You were honestly probably one of the first people to hear about this concept as it was still taking shape in one of its earliest conceptual stages. Thank you so much!

My editor/proofreader, and long time partner Kaylynn, who is my sounding board to most of the nonsense I conjure up when my brain does *the thing*. You're oftentimes a captive audience and I feel sorry for her for having to endure some of my ridiculous ideas. But ... not *all* of them are so crazy. I'm thankful for you and I love you. You da bomb.

Amy Tackett. My Religious and Bible authenticity guide. Amy, you were a huge help with keeping me honest and asking me questions around the topics of denomination and whatnot. I am super grateful to have had you as a consultant with this story. Also, thank you so much for being one of the beta readers. Your input and willingness to challenge me in all areas only contributed to making this a more complete and stronger story, even if you drive a Jeep.

A.W. Mason. What can I say about this guy? Incredible author (Seriously, go read *Judy Martin's Final Curtain Call*). You're someone I respect in the field and I am lucky to call you a friend and lean on for anything I've asked of you with writing stuff. Your help with the beta reading phase of this proves to be pivotal in how this book ultimately shaped up. Calling me out on areas that could be beefed up and then just sharing your knowledge that—to me—feels like I should have known, but I am glad to have eventually learned through this. Big thanks, my dude!

A special thanks to Willie R. Heredia. Thanks for beta reading and helping clean up some of the messy things that I didn't know were messy. I am looking forward to your future work and returning the favor as a beta reader.

Christy Aldridge at Grim Poppy Design. Despite my pickiness with the vision, you were super easy to work with and handled the design like a total pro. I can't say enough good things. I'll keep pointing people in your direction.

Big thanks to Joey Powell for the interior formatting (thanks for making the guts pretty). Joey not only writes wild stories with a flare of originality, but he also does a little bit of everything. Your entrepreneurial spirit and ability to be a resource for everyone has proven to be invaluable and I'm rooting for you my dude. Your talent is only matched by your kindness.

I need to thank Mo Medusa for looking over excerpts I shared, even at times when I just needed validation probably, and also additional insight. Mo has become an unofficial critique partner in ways and I consider myself lucky to know you. I enjoy your friendship and being able to just riff about ideas and see where they go.

Ali Anthanasiou, thank you for once again being a beta reader for another one of my silly stories. Your insight is always something I look forward to when I reach the finish line for publishing something because you are always so thorough and thoughtful with your feedback and I always have something to take away from it after. I can only hope that someone steals this book from your Little Free Library and hopefully enjoys it. Thank you again.

Nico Bell, Author and editor. Thank you for being a beta reader. I know it was a last minute thing but I appreciate your timely feedback and honest input. Static Screams is awesome and I'm looking forward to watching your author journey and seeing what you do next.

And finally.

You.

Thank you so much for reading this book. It will never feel normal to me that anyone reads my work and I am incredibly grateful for you.

About The Author

David lives in the Greater Cincinnati area (in Northern Kentucky for any locals who choose to argue about geography) where he lives with his two teen sons and the lady of the house. When David isn't fighting imposter syndrome as a writer he is probably working out, watching horror movies, baseball, or wrestling.

Suspense and Tension are David's playground and he has independently self-published multiple books in addition to having short stories published in several anthologies.

<u>Other Published Works</u>

Novels

Devils That Prey

Novellas

The Tickle Monster

Features

HorrorScope: A Zodiac Anthology, Vol.2.

Curbside Curses: The Yardsale Anthology

Stay connected with David Washburn.
Say "hello."

www.WashburnWrites.com
Instagram | Threads
@WashburnWrites

www.ingramcontent.com/pod-product-compliance
Lightning Source LLC
Chambersburg PA
CBHW021547310726
48972CB00003B/708